Brockton lives with his wife, Sonia; and their three children, Alyssa, Adrienne and Joseph, in beautiful Vaughan, Ontario, Canada. He is a very proud Canadian. When not teaching, he enjoys reading and crafting stories. He gets his inspiration from listening to his elders sharing magical, adventurous tales that were once told to them by their elders. Brockton dreams his stories and writes his dreams. He likes to travel and has a weakness for different foods. He claims to stop eating only when his arms get tired. His wish is that his writing puts a smile on every reader's face.

UNDER THE OLIVE TREE
Literary Creations

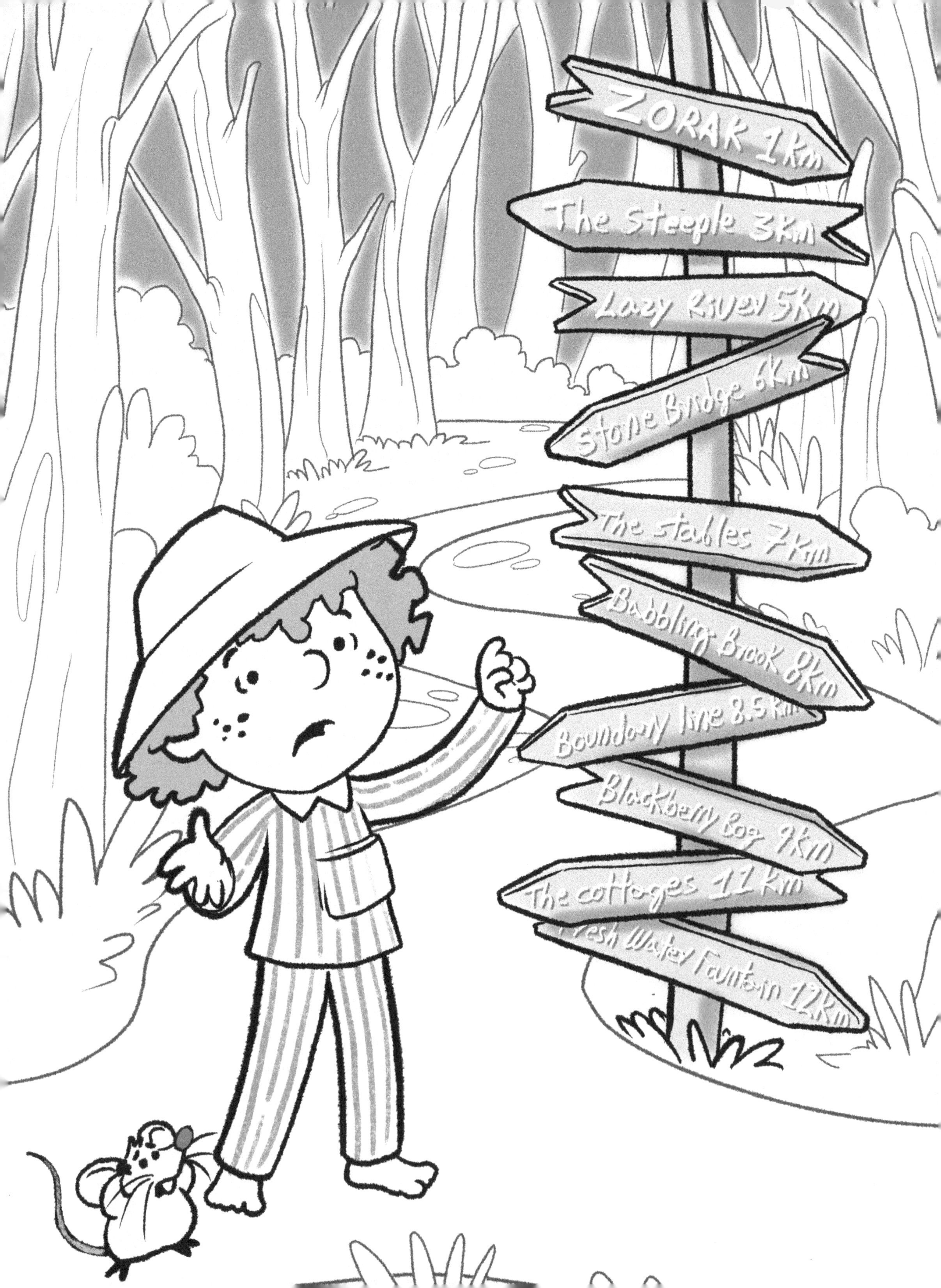
ZORAK 1Km
The Steeple 3Km
Lazy River 5Km
Stone Bridge 6Km
The stables 7Km
Babbling Brook 8Km
Boundary line 8.5Km
Blackberry Bog 9Km
The cottages 11Km
Fresh Water Fountain 12Km

The Tale of the Missing Tail

Brockton Moutray

AUSTIN MACAULEY PUBLISHERS™

LONDON * CAMBRIDGE * NEW YORK * SHARJAH

Copyright © Brockton Moutray (2020)

A CIP catalogue record for this title is available from the British Library.

ISBN 9781528908351 (Paperback)
ISBN 9781528958905 (ePub e-book)

www.austinmacauley.com

First Published (2020)
Austin Macauley Publishers Ltd
25 Canada Square
Canary Wharf
London
E14 5LQ

This book is dedicated to my wife and children.

Table of Contents

Grandpa's Farm

In a lush green valley, not too far from here, lived a ten-year-old boy named Joseph Logan. Joseph lived on his grandpa's farm with his mother and father and three older brothers Seth, Jacob and Jeremiah. Curly carrot-coloured hair sprung out from under Joseph's straw hat, and his deep blue eyes always sparkled. Everyone joked about his size. He was definitely the smallest ten-year-old in the valley. He was so small for his age that his father would often jokingly say to him, "Son, you better fill your pockets with some rocks. We wouldn't want a gust of wind carrying our little Joseph away."

Everyone joked about his smile, missing two front teeth.

Everyone loved Joseph. Joseph had many friends. Some of his friends, like Noah Toppleberry, his best friend, who sat beside him in class, called him Tadpole on account of his size. Others, like Emma Lapis, the pretty little girl in his class with the beautiful green eyes and the rosy cheeks—both he and Noah had a crush on her—called him G.I Joe on account of the khaki-coloured shorts he wore with the sewn-in army logo. At school, Joseph always stared at Emma who he thought was as cute as a button, but he always caught bug-eyed Noah staring at her too. Joseph, making sure that Miss Cameron couldn't hear, would nudge Noah and whisper, "Hey, stop staring at her. Emma's mine, all mine! You got it Noah? You just stop staring at her." Noah would stare at Joseph through his thick, wire-rimmed glasses and smirk.

Joseph loved to read. He often sat alone on the stonewall at the far end of the meadow under the cool shade of the giant maple tree and read stories about tiny fairies that caused all sorts of mischief, and grumpy ogres that lived under rickety bridges, and crafty gingerbread men who could run and talk, and ancient wizards with long white beards who cast all sorts of magical spells, and plump pink pigs that could build houses out of straw, and friendly fire-breathing dragons that could fly, and enchanted forests that could sing, and pretty damsels in distress who waited nervously in damp dungeons for brave knights in shining armour to save them from evil villains. Joseph especially loved stories ending with, "...and they lived happily ever after."

Grandpa's farmhouse lay in the middle of a meadow of golden wheat high on a plateau nestled between forested rolling hills. On one side of the meadow, nearer the house, potatoes grew, and on the far side, onions. "Onions can't be planted too close to the potatoes," his grandpa once told Joseph, "'cause they make taters cry their eyes out." Joseph loved his grandpa because Grandpa always made him chuckle.

Every morning Joseph stared out his bedroom window and watched the white-winged mourning doves cuddle and coo along the wooden fence that bordered the meadow. He watched the Grey squirrels scurry across Ma's clothesline, looking like the bearded acrobats who performed every year at the County Fair. He always dreamed of the weekend, of fishing with Grandpa and his brothers along the river or of passing the warm lazy days skipping flat rocks with his friends or of building castles with river rocks. Every morning he waited by his bedroom window until Ma shouted, "Come and get it, boys. Breakfast is ready, you sleepy heads. Rise and shine, rise and shine. Hurry. You don't want to be late for school." Joseph loved living on his grandpa's farm, loved waking early, and loved going to school to see Emma Lapis.

Cute as a Button

Joseph sat in his desk at school daydreaming about Emma Lapis. The shuffling of feet under desks and the creak, creak, creak of the floorboards, the rustling of paper and the scratching of lead pencils on newsprint and the zippy voice and tap, tap, tap of Miss Cameron's heels filled the classroom.

Joseph listened to the familiar sounds for a moment and then closed his math book. He slid his hand into the right pocket of his khaki-overalls. Gingerly glancing over his right shoulder, he scanned the classroom looking for Emma. He nudged Noah sitting next to him.

"She's mine, Noah!" Joseph whispered.

Noah peeped over his left shoulder at Joseph. "No, she's not! She's—she's—she's mine, Tadpole." He leaned back on the bench and whispered, "Keep your voice down. Do you want Miss Cameron to—to—to—have a fit?"

Miss Cameron rhythmically recited the seven times table. "Seven times five is thirty-five, seven times six is forty-two, seven times seven is forty-nine..."

Her footsteps creaked and echoed as she paced back and forth along and between the rows of desks. The students made eye contact with Miss Cameron as they recited their math lesson in unison, making sure to enunciate every syllable.

"That's it. Very good! Keep pace, everyone. Don't rush. Nice and clear. Picture the numbers as you say them. Seven times eight is fifty-six..."

She stopped in front of Lauren, a freckled-face, red-hair girl who always smiled, giggled, and joked around. Lauren sat in the row behind Joseph and spent most of the day staring at him and passing silly notes to him when no one was looking. Miss Cameron tapped a finger on Lauren's desk to the beat of the times table. "Seven times nine is sixty-three, seven times ten is seventy."

"I—I—I know my times table and you—you—you don't," Noah whispered to Joseph, keeping his eyes fixed on his math book.

Joseph kicked Noah's leg and whispered back, "Yes, I do. All of it! I can probably say it quicker than you. Miss Cameron even told Ma I would pass math this year."

"Why, slap my head and call me stupid," Noah responded, his voice rising. "I'll definitely pass all the grade five subjects and—and—and I'll be sitting right beside Emma next year... so there!"

"And—and—and," Joseph mimicked Noah. "Is that all you can say? At least I don't stammer. Miss Cameron told Ma that I would be next to erase the chalkboard...so there!"

"You're so small you—you—you can't even *reach* the chalkboard."

"Yes, I can."

"No, you can't and—and—and besides, next week is Lauren's turn. You're a—a—a liar."

"No, I'm not!"

"Yes, you are and—and—and you're so short I bet Emma doesn't even know you exist."

"Sure she does!" Joseph's voice grew louder, drawing the attention of Miss Cameron.

"She was the first at school this morning and she held the door open for me."

"Keep your voice down or we'll get into a—a—a heap of trouble. Emma held it open for me too. She's this week's classroom monitor so—so—so she gets to hold the door and—and—and—and—and to erase the chalkboard."

Miss Cameron strolled to the side of the class and gave Joseph and Noah a stern, disapproving look.

"You think you're better than everyone, don't you?" Joseph whispered.

"You're just jealous."

"No. I'm not."

"Yes you are. And—and—and I won the potato sack race yesterday and you didn't even finish and—and—and Miss Cameron sent me to sharpen the pencils twice this week. Did she ever pick you?"

"So?" Joseph slammed his book down on the bench, now fully attracting the teacher's attention. "I got picked to stand at the front of the class and sing the national anthem."

"So what?" Noah snatched the pencil from Joseph's hand and scribbled, "Emma likes Noah!" across the page of Joseph's math book.

"No she doesn't, stupid head!" huffed Joseph, frantically erasing the words.

Miss Cameron raised her hand in the air and the students stopped reciting the times table. She fixed her eyeglasses on the bridge of her nose and glared across the first rows of desks. "Boys, are you preparing to recite the two times table or are you too busy with something else?"

"No, Miss. I mean, yes Miss," Joseph replied, keeping his eyes glued to his math book.

"We're ready when you are, Miss Cameron," he added, forcing a smile.

"Boys, please pay attention and don't interrupt!" Miss Cameron turned, cleared her throat and addressed the students. "Good work! Now open your notebooks and write the six times table, four times. Dismissal will be in fifteen minutes."

Joseph shuffled in his seat. He turned around and peered past Lauren and the rows of students to Emma. She sat on the bench with both feet planted firmly on the floor. Her long auburn hair brushed against her dark blue pinafore, cascaded down her white starched blouse, and fell onto her reader. Emma's head was low to the desk and cocked slightly to the left. Her green eyes move left-right, left-right as they followed the arithmetic. She stopped writing and lifted her head, as if she could feel someone was looking her way, and her eyes met Joseph's. Emma blushed and moved her left hand over her mouth. Her two best friends, Brooke Wheeler and Katie Simpleton, noticed Joseph's stare. Katie kicked Emma's leg under the desk and giggled. Emma lowered her eyes and placed her hand back on her notebook. The silver pin on the lapel of her pinafore shimmered in the late afternoon sunshine.

Miss Cameron glanced up at the clock and then paced closer to the front of the classroom.

Joseph stared at Emma and rested his cheek on the back of the chair. "She's as pretty as a button," he said to himself. "I wonder if she likes me." He leaned over to Noah. "Is it almost dismissal?"

"Shhh! She's—she's—she's coming."

Miss Cameron rapped her yardstick on Joseph's desk. "Joseph, how many times must I remind you that we sit with our backs straight with both feet on the ground?"

"Yes, Miss. Excuse me, Miss."

"Now please sit up and pay attention, young man. You've done enough talking for one day. We still have a few minutes before dismissal. Why don't you and your friend Noah recite the three times table for me?"

"Yes, Miss. I'm sorry."

Miss Cameron adjusted her wire-rimmed glasses and tapped her yardstick on the floor.

"Three times one is three, three times two is six, and three times three is nine. Remember, enunciate every word and picture the numbers as you say them." She faced the chalkboard and listened as Noah and Joseph rhythmically recited the times table and then joined in while keeping beat with her yardstick. "... and three times ten is thirty."

"Okay everyone," she said, turning to address the entire class. "Let's make sure that our books are placed neatly inside our desktops and that our desks are cleared. Emma, you're this week's monitor, so please go erase the boards and then please hold the door open for everyone." Emma's cheeks turned red. Giggles and chatter filled the schoolhouse. The dismissal bell rang. "Remember, everyone stops and genuflects in front of the crucifix before leaving. Have a good afternoon everyone."

"Good afternoon, Miss Cameron," the entire class responded in unison.

Warm, hazy afternoon sunlight filled the back of the schoolhouse as Emma swung opened the classroom door. Ladybugs took flight and buzzed over the top of the students' heads before escaping outdoors to the shade under the maple trees that lined the cobblestone path. The path wound gently down the hill, past the playground, and to the rusty front iron-gate.

"Come on, Tadpole! Are you coming Tadpole?"

"You go ahead, Noah. I'll be out in a few minutes. I just have to put my books in my knapsack and put the chair up on my desk," Joseph responded, hoping that Noah would leave so he could speak to Emma alone.

Noah ran to the open door, stopped, smiled at Emma and said, "Bye Emma, have—have—have a nice day. See you—you—you on Monday." He exited the school, his cheeks aflame.

Once Joseph figured that Noah was past the iron-gate, he picked up his knapsack and ambled towards the opened door, hoping to speak to Emma. His mind raced with things that he might say to impress her, but as he ambled to the door his lips remained pursed together and his tongue remained stuck to the roof of his mouth. He could feel his knees rattling as he passed Emma. "Have a great weekend, G.I. Joe," said Emma. Tongue-tied and downcast eyes, he waved his hand in the air and lumbered down the path.

Joseph had missed his chance to speak to Emma alone. He turned up along the riverbank towards home muttering, "How foolish of me. I had Emma all alone. Just her and I and no one else. No Noah, no Brooke Wheeler, no Katie Simpleton, no Miss Cameron...nobody. I blew it! I missed my chance to speak to Emma alone. I'm dumber than a bag of nails... geez!" he said, slapping his straw hat against his knee.

After ambling along the river for over one hour thinking of what he could have said to Emma, had he found the courage to do so, he finally stepped onto the front stoop of the farmhouse and sat down on the top step to regain his composure. Adjusting the straw hat on his head, he placed a reed between his teeth and walked to the kitchen.

"And where have you been, young man?" said his mother, carefully hanging a black pot over the glowing embers in the hearth. "Sorry, Ma. I guess I lost track of the time."

"Well, you get down into that chicken coop and help your brothers finish scattering corn, filling the drinking wells, and checking for freshly-laid eggs. Then, you get cleaned up and come straight to dinner, understood? We're having Grandpa's favourite tonight, rabbit stew. Now get! I'm expecting you and your brothers back in ten minutes!"

"Yes, Ma. I'll be back in a wink."

Over at the chicken coop, Jacob, Jeremiah and Seth taunted and whistled at Joseph as he helped them complete the chores. Joseph paid little attention to their brickbats.

"So how was school today, Tadpole? Everything okay between you and that pretty, little, rich, city slicker?" Jacob teased. "Does Lauren know you have a crush on Emma?"

"Did pretty little Miss Teacher's Pet hold the door open for you, Tadpole? I saw her lean over and give you a big wet kiss," Jeremiah mocked.

"I tried getting a good look at Emma kissing bug-eyed Noah Toppleberry by the river today, but the sunlight was glinting off her shiny patent leather shoes and I almost lost my eyesight," Seth chimed in, grabbing Joseph in a headlock and rubbing the top of his head with his knuckles. Then he sang, "Noah and Emma sitting in a tree, k-i-s-s-i-n-g. First comes love, then comes marriage, then comes Noah's and Emma's baby in a baby carriage."

The boys cheered and laughed. They ran out of the chicken coop to the front stoop, stopped to composed themselves and calmly filed into the kitchen ready for dinner.

An Extra-Special Saturday

Today was Saturday. Today was the day that Grandpa Logan had promised Joseph that he would let him in on a little secret. Joseph loved secrets. He sat on the stonewall at the far end of the meadow anxiously waiting for Grandpa, thinking what on earth his secret could possibly be. He felt special knowing that Grandpa was going to share his secret with him. Today was an extra-special Saturday because it was the day before his eighth birthday.

"Are you ready, Joseph?"

"Ready, Grandpa!" Joseph followed Grandpa along the bank of the river that snaked through Grandpa's farm and disappeared down into the lush valley below. He stayed near Grandpa, knowing that if he got too close to the edge, the ground would give way and he'd slip into the water. Joseph struggled to keep pace. He had never been so deep in the valley.

"Grandpa, where are we going?"

"Just keep up, Joseph. It's a secret."

"I love secrets, Grandpa!"

As Joseph and Grandpa strolled along the trail, they passed the limestone bluffs of Muddy River until they reached a deep dark valley between two high ridges. Every now and then, Joseph's eyes fell from Grandpa in front of him to the beauty of the gorge. Joseph felt like an explorer in a mysterious valley. They came upon a narrow horse trail that dipped down into a little hollow fringed with mulberries and holly. The ground was moist, the air heavy. Joseph fell behind. He removed his straw hat and swiped his forehead with his forearm. His t-shirt stuck to his body. Grandpa, as if he had eyes in the back of his head, turned, saying, "Come Joseph, keep up, we're almost there." Joseph scampered to catch up with Grandpa, whose shirt was stained with sweat, his tanned fedora swinging in his right hand.

"Grandpa, I'm right behind you," he shouted, patting the straw hat back on his head. "Are we almost there?"

Grandpa pointed ahead, turning his back to Joseph. "Just over this ridge, Joseph." They mounted the hill and reached an enormous rock face that stretched far up into the sky. "Rest for a spell on that there log, Joseph. I remember leaving a lantern behind that boulder over yonder," Grandpa said, wiping sweat from his brow. "I think we'll need it. I'll be right back."

"I sure am plumb worn out," Joseph admitted. Exhausted, excited, and a little hungry, Joseph dangled his feet over the mossy ground and watched as Grandpa searched for the tin lantern. Grandpa struck a wooden match against the rock face, found the coalminer's lantern, and lit it. A hazy yellow light glowed in the dark forest.

"Here you go, Joseph. You hang on to this." Joseph took the lantern from Grandpa and followed him into a cavern. "Don't be afraid. Do you remember the dream I once told you about?"

"Is this the place, Grandpa? Is this where you came to dig for treasure when you were a little boy?"

"Yes, this is the place—my secret cave. Only you and I know. It's *our* secret, Joseph."

"Wow! Our very own secret and our very own secret cave!" declared Joseph, marvelling at his surroundings.

Joseph treaded behind Grandpa, carrying the old tin lantern in his right hand. The dim light of the cave's entrance slowly vanished as they ventured lower and further through a narrow shaft. The shrill cry of cave crickets and the flutter of bats echoed throughout the dark cavern. Joseph's mind swam with images of pirates risking their lives on adventurous journeys in search of buried treasures, brave knights clashing with magical monsters saving princesses locked up in mighty stone dungeons, and wise wizards appearing and disappearing amid puffs of smoke.

"Come Joseph, don't be afraid." Grandpa's voice startled Joseph back to reality. The lantern cast shadows on the cavern walls and a million spangles of light on the ground. Grandpa pulled out a small paper bag and a broken piece of clay roof tile from his trouser pockets. He scraped the tile against the cavern wall until the paper bag overflowed with coarse white sand.

"Is that sand magic?" Joseph asked.

"I suppose it could be."

"Why do you collect it, Grandpa?"

"Your ma buries garbanzo beans in this sand and then roasts them in the fire pit. They're simply delicious. You'll see. Ma's preparing them tonight, for dinner."

"Wow! Magic garbanzo beans, Grandpa?"

"I suppose they could be."

"Did you ever find any buried treasure, Grandpa?"

"No. Perhaps one day you'll find it. Come. Let's get back home. Your dad should be back soon. Besides, I'm getting hungry, aren't you?"

Joseph swung the oil lantern and stared at the spangles dancing and flickering on the cavern walls and floors. As Grandpa carried the bag of magic sand out of the cavern, Joseph wondered whether pirates, wizards, dragons, ogres or fairies had once lived in this cavern—perhaps a million years ago. Joseph quietly followed Grandpa along the horse trail, through the hollow, between the rock bluffs, along the river, up the slope to the large willow tree, through the pumpkin patch, and past the fire pit. They could see the sun setting behind the farmhouse. The donkey brayed under the apple tree by the shed, the pot-bellied pig grunted in the pen beside the silo and the crickets cried in the meadow of golden wheat.

Grandpa sat down in his rocking chair on the front stoop by the clay jar. Joseph rested the lantern on the ground and climbed onto Grandpa's lap. A gentle breeze rattled the wind chime, tingling and jingling and clinking. A red-winged blackbird, as if wanting to join in on the conversation, swooped down from the clothesline and perched itself on the lip of a galvanized bucket by the window next to the rocking chair.

"Grandpa?"

"Yes, Joseph."

"Do you believe in magic?"

"Absolutely—as much as I believe in the moon, the sun, and the stars!"

Joseph looked up at the moon in the eastern sky and then fixed his eyes on the small bag of magical sand. "Good. So do I, Grandpa. So do I." The blackbird fluttered back to the clothesline. "Are you hungry, Grandpa?"

"I could eat a horse." Grandpa chuckled, rose from the rocking chair with Joseph in his arms, and turned towards the farm house's front door. Joseph had three things on his mind as Grandpa carried him inside—the secret cavern, the magical garbanzo beans, and pretty Emma Lapis.

That evening, Joseph sat opposite Grandpa at the dinner table, exchanging glances. Each understood what the other was thinking. Grandpa's eyes flitted around the table before winking at Joseph and mouthing the word "magical" between forkfuls of roasted garbanzo beans sprinkled with paprika and coarse salt. Grandpa smiled and pressed his fingers to his lips instructing Joseph to keep the cavern and the magic garbanzo beans a guarded secret. Joseph winked back at Grandpa, acknowledging their mutual pledge of silence. He paid no heed to the others and continued eating the delicious roasted beans, thinking of Emma and the possibility of one day finding buried treasure.

That evening, Joseph tossed and turned under his blanket, one minute feeling cold and clammy, the next feeling warm and feverish. He had eaten far too many roasted garbanzo beans. His head raced with images of spangled light and dark shadows dancing on the walls of Grandpa's secret cavern. His head resounded with the shrill cry of crickets and the flutter of bats, flashed with pirates and wizards and dragons and ogres and fairies trying to leap out from the pages of his story book, flooded with the images of bug-eyed Noah ogling his girl Emma Lapis, and filled with the secretive glances of Grandpa at the dinner table. Joseph flipped over onto his rumbling, grumbling tummy and slipped his arms under his pillow. Although his eyelids grew heavy, his head felt light, and his arms leaden, Joseph was unable to sleep.

A Falling Star

Too shaken to go back to sleep, Joseph lay awake staring out his bedroom window at the bright stars twinkling in the night sky. He listened to the loud, high-pitched singing of the crickets in the field. He thought back to Emma blushing, to Noah stammering through the times table, to the spangles of light dancing on the cavern wall, to his brothers' laughter and jeers in the chicken coop, to the enchanted places he explored in his comic books, and especially to the delicious, magic garbanzo beans roasted in the fire pit.

Joseph spotted a distant star arching through the night sky, a trail of dazzling stardust glittering in its wake. He got out of bed, shook the cobwebs out of his head, and leaned against the windowsill, his nose pressed up against the pane. He crossed his fingers and made a wish. "Star light, star bright, the first star I see tonight; I wish I may, I wish I might, have the wish I wish tonight." He watched the falling star slowly fade into the darkness and finally disappear behind the old apple tree in the middle of Grandpa's meadow. Joseph yawned and slid back into bed. He pulled the wool blanket over his head, rolled onto his belly, and tucked his arms under his pillow. He drifted off when his left leg suddenly jerked forward, as if he were falling, and woke up. Joseph opened his eyes wide, and he found himself standing barefoot in his striped pyjamas on a cool dirt floor. He shivered and adjusted his eyes to the darkness.

"Where am I?" he said in a sleepy voice. "Seth, Jacob, Jeremiah, are you here? Hello, is anybody here?"

A chill ran up Joseph's spine and goose bumps blanketed his arms. He wrapped his arms around his shoulders. "Hello? Pa, Ma, Grandpa? Is anybody here?" He saw a faint glowing light to his right, behind what appeared to be a large rock. Joseph carefully stepped around the rock. Joseph bent down and picked up his grandfather's lit coal miner's lantern. He lifted it high above his head. "I'm in Grandpa's secret cave!" He shuffled his feet, wiggled his toes, and announced with excitement, "I know you're here, Grandpa. Hello? Where are you, Grandpa?" The lantern in Joseph's hand swung back and forth as he paced and waited for Grandpa's approaching shadow. He looked around at the colourful spangles of light dancing on the cavern walls. "Grandpa, are you here looking for buried treasure again?" he said. "Come out, come out, wherever you are," he said in a sing-song voice.

Moving the lantern away from his body as far as he could, Joseph peered across the cavern through the yellow glow stained with darkness, anxiously awaiting for a response. He remained perfectly still, looked to his left and then to his right, sighed, and laid the lantern on the ground beside him. He removed his straw hat and scratched his head.

"How did I get here? I remember eating garbanzo beans.... No, I was lying in bed. No I wasn't, I was waking up from a terrible dream. No I wasn't. I was standing by the window watching a star streak across the sky and fall into Grandpa's meadow. I remember humming 'Star light, star bright, the first star I see tonight; I wish I may, I wish I might, have the wish I wish tonight.' Wait, now I remember. I was turning on my tummy and sliding my arms under my pillow... I think?"

Joseph put his hat back on and bent down and picked up the lantern. He tiptoed through the cavern searching for an entrance while trying to figure out how on earth he ended up inside the dark cavern. He retraced his journey with Grandpa from the cave back to the farmhouse—down the horse trail, through the hollow, between the rock bluffs, along the river, up the slope to the willow tree, through the pumpkin patch, and past the fire pit. "Golly, I hope there's enough oil in this here lantern to get me back home."

Joseph felt the ground give out from under him. The cavern dirt floor crumbled and he fell straight down a narrow, sandy shaft—whoosh! Down, down, down he fell. His haunches brushed against the bumpy shaft walls. He let go of the lantern. His hat flew off his head and his hair stood on end as he dropped faster and faster down the dark shaft. "Wee!" Joseph screamed as if he were on a carnival ride at the agricultural fair. The shaft widened into a tunnel. Joseph continued to sail freely in midair.

"Oh me! Oh my!" He toppled head over heels, his arms swinging wildly in every direction. "Help! Help!"

He bumped into a rickety old free-floating chair. Joseph's bum landed on the seat and he grabbed at the sides of the chair to hold himself firmly in place. His body stopped tumbling but still he plummeted down the tunnel in the chair. He shook his head to try to regain focus and stop the world from spinning.

"Hey, watch where you're going young man!" shouted a crooked old man holding a big fat cat in one arm, and shaking a gnarly finger. Joseph stretched an arm to the side to try to grab something to stop his fall, all the while plunging down the tunnel on the chair like a falling dart at an alarming speed. He managed to bring his arms down and then stuff his hands into his pyjama pockets.

"Oh me! I shouldn't have done that," he said. The chair got away from him and bounced off the tunnel wall. "Help!"

Joseph began to top-spin farther and farther down the tunnel. "Won't someone help me? Noah? Emma? Someone! Please help! Pretty please! Pretty please, with sugar on top!"

He fell so fast he couldn't hear his own voice. Warm air rushed up his legs and filled his pyjamas. Then suddenly, as if his plea had been answered, Joseph found himself floating calmly, like an escaped balloon in mid-air.

"I know!" He scratched his head, wondering why he hadn't thought of it before. "It's the garbanzo beans Ma roasted! Of course! I must be having another crazy dream."

Still suspended, Joseph controlled his movements as though he were swimming in the creek by Grandpa's house. He laughed hysterically. "What a fool I am! This ain't for real.

It's just a dream. I reckon I ate too many of those magical garbanzo beans." He looked up and then down and continued to laugh. "I wish bug-eyed Noah could see me now! He'd be so jealous."

A tiny old wizard wearing cowboy boots and spurs, saddling a striped bumblebee in a bubble the size of a cantaloupe floated past Joseph. The wizard held a sign that read, "Hello there. My name is Scribbles. What's yours?"

"My name is Joseph, but my family and friends call me Sprout," Joseph shouted as he floated like a soap bubble farther and farther past the wizard riding the bumblebee. He stared down past his bare feet and spotted a brilliant white light far below. "Jeepers, this sure is a strange dream! I wish I were in my soft bed right now. I'd rather be sucking on a sour lemon than floating aimlessly in this never-ending tunnel!"

Joseph slowly descended into the brilliant white light. He stared at a large dish holding hands with a tall spoon. They both wore running shoes and ran along the tunnel walls shouting, "Hurry, hurry, before someone sees us!" Joseph waved his hands in the air to try and get their attention. They ignored him. The bright light engulfed his toes, swept over his feet, covered his ankles, swathed his legs, and then swaddled his entire body. Joseph floated serenely through the shaft of white light. He nosedived down, did three summersaults, swam back up, and then spun like a top.

"Is anybody down here?" he shouted.

"Yes, we're all here, *absolutely*."

Joseph squinted down through the bright light and saw that the voice came from a ladybug holding a polka-dotted umbrella floating freely in the tunnel. A green goose wearing a bowtie flew above the ladybug, honking, "Cross now…cross now!"

"Hey my favourite hat! Where did you come from?" Joseph reached up and grabbed his tattered straw hat that drifted calmly above his head. He tapped the hat firmly back on his head and continued to float freely. He pursed his lips, rubbed his chin, and furrowed his brow.

"If I wake up, I'll find myself in my soft, comfy bed and this will all be over… *if* this is all a dream. If this is *not* a dream, then I'll probably float around up here until I hit the ground… *if* there's ground down below. And *if* I do hit ground, where will I end up?" He looked up, then down past his toes. "Will someone be down there to help me back to Grandpa's farm?" he shouted. "Will I ever see my family again? Will I ever see Emma again? How will I get back? I simply must get back home. If I don't, Ma will go looking for me in the morning. If I don't, the desk beside Noah will be empty and what will Miss Cameron think—that I'm playing hooky? That I'm at home, sick? Hello, is anybody down there? Grandpa? I must get back home before Emma falls in love with that black-beetle-eyed-stammering-good-for-nothing-Noah, and then they'll get married, and then they'll…. Oh me, oh my! What on earth can I do?"

Joseph pinched his nose and then slapped his cheeks. "Wake up Joseph! Wake up

Joseph! Come on G.I. Joe! It's back to school tomorrow! Emma will be waiting." He crossed his fingers on both hands and placed them behind his back, shut his eyes, and counted backwards from ten, hoping he'd be back in his bed when he opened them. "Ten—nine—eight—seven—six—five—four—three..."

Joseph fluttered his eyelids to sneak a peek and saw six monkeys smoking cigars. He quickly shifted his weight to avoid bumping into them. "Hey, look out!"

He shut his eyes again and finished counting "two—and—one!" He opened them, looked up, and saw six monkeys jeering at him as they floated aimlessly above him in the bright light. "I can't believe what I'm seeing! Seth? Jacob? Jeremiah? Can someone please help me?"

The farther Joseph floated down the tunnel, the cooler the air. Suddenly his pyjama bottoms began to deflate.

Joseph wrapped his arms around his shivering shoulders. "I sure wish I had my wool blanket. I'd gladly trade my *Snakes and Ladders* game for a wool blanket right about now." Joseph rifled faster and faster down the tunnel again. He closed his eyes and counted backwards from twenty, hoping again to be back in bed when he opened them. "Twenty—nineteen—eighteen—seventeen—sixteen—fifteen—fourteen—thirteen—twelve—eleven—ten—"

"Did you say *Snakes and Ladders*? It's definitely my all-time favourite board game!" Joseph looked around and saw that the voice was coming from a colourful jack-in-the-box sprung open and waving at him. "Hello there, young man," the jack-in-the-box said in a chipper voice. "You might want to slow down about now before you hit the bottom."

The cold air turned frigid and snowflakes fluttered and danced around Joseph. He ignored the jack-in-the-box and started counting again. "Nine—eight—seven—six... " He flipped up the collar of his pyjama top. His lips turned blue as the sea and his nose red as a tomato. "Ah heck, it's no use. Why did I have to go and eat so many garbanzo beans last night?"

Then his fall slowed down as suddenly as it sped up. A spiny warthog wearing a red bandana around its head, sneakers on its back hooves, and boxing gloves on its front hooves moved by. "Left jab. Left jab followed by a right upper cut," the warthog shouted as it shadowboxed.

Whoosh! Wham! Whomp! Whump!

"Hey, what's going on?"

Joseph was dumped out of a round, sloped opening at the bottom of the tunnel, and he bumped and scraped and rolled and slid down a steep mountain ridge covered in snow. He tucked his left hand under his right armpit, and with his right hand, held onto his straw hat. "Look out below!" he hollered.

He gathered speed as he barrelled faster and faster down the mountain, dodging large boulders, sliding over frozen streams and under giant cedars, and ploughing through snow banks.

"Help, help!"

The snow beneath him disappeared and he rolled like a barrel down a steep cliff, bumping and scraping along the ground. "Grandpa, where are you? Help!"

Is Anybody Home?

Joseph lay on his back with his legs up in the air pressed against a wooden fence. He stared up into an unfamiliar blue sky with a dumbfounded expression on his face.

"Am I still alive?"

With only a few bumps and bruises, Joseph staggered slowly to his feet and dusted snow and dirt off him. "Am I still dreaming?" He pinched his nose and then slapped his cheeks.

"Rats!" he cried out when he realized that he was not in his bed. "Double-rats!" he shouted when he discovered the straw hat no longer sat on his head.

He sighed and picked leaves and twigs out of his hair. He moaned, gingerly turning to his left and to his right. "Hello, is anybody here? Can anybody tell me where I am?" He adjusted his pyjamas. "This certainly ain't Grandpa's farm!"

Joseph rubbed his palms together and stared in awe up at massive snow-capped mountains that towered high into the sky, with some peaks stretching into the heavens and disappearing above the white clouds. "Those ain't the rolling hills around Grandpa's farm, that's for sure!" He winced in pain as he massaged his aching neck and shoulders. "Jeepers that was some fall!"

He looked back up and saw jagged cliffs, smooth rock faces, regal blue pine and clusters of cypress trees blanketing the majestic mountain range.

"Did I fall from the sky and slide down them there mountains? Wow!"

Joseph took a few steps forward and squinted at a cluster of shimmering, sun baked, red-clay roofs atop a series of staggered terraces of olive trees, lemon trees, and vineyards. His eyes followed them as they climbed along the hillside to whitewashed stone houses.

"These ain't farmhouses like back home. They look like scattered crates piled one on top of the next and they even lean against each other." He scratched his chin. "Why, if one toppled over, they'd all come tumbling down like dominoes."

He began the long trek up the hillside, hoping to find someone who could help him find his way back to Grandpa's farm. The air was laden with the pungent scent of lemons. Beyond the cluster of houses, he spotted a tall stone structure leaning to the right and glistening in the sun.

"Is that a steeple?" Joseph wondered. "Yes, it is a steeple—there's the church." He thought of a plan. "If I go to the church and open the door, perhaps I'll find people. If nobody's in the church, then I'll bet there's someone in that there steeple."

A short, stout Billy Goat with a long white beard stepped out from behind a bush. "Where are you going?" it said in a gruff voice. Joseph didn't hear it. "I'm speaking to you, Pyjama Boy!"

23

Joseph jumped back startled and gaped at the goat. "It can't be...I must still be dreaming!"

"I asked you a question, young man, and I expect a response—is that clear?" The Billy Goat butted its head against a fallen log.

"I'm only ten, but I definitely know that goats can't talk," Joseph declared, shaking his head.

"Listen, Pyjama Boy. This goat does talk, and I want an answer! Where are you going?"

Joseph grinned at the goat and then laughed. "Please don't be upset with me, but no one has ever called me Pyjama Boy." His smile turned to a frown. "I'm lost, I think. I was going to that church to ask for help. I'm trying to get back to Grandpa's farm."

"If you go near the steeple, you'll be sorry. Old Man Wilbur lives there and he eats little boys for breakfast, little girls for lunch, and anyone else he can find for dinner."

"Golly! I'm speaking to a goat—a real, honest-to-goodness goat. Emma would love to see this!"

"Yes, you are speaking to a goat, and if you don't listen to me, you'll be tonight's dinner, you foolish little Pyjama Boy."

Joseph stepped closer to the goat. "Can you please tell me where I am? And, what's your name?"

"What is *my* name? You tell me *your* name first. You, after all, are the stranger around here."

"Yes, yes of course." Joseph was taken aback from being scolded by a talking Billy Goat. "My name is Joseph, but my family and friends call me Sprout, and some call me G.I. Joe on account of my khaki-coloured overalls with the army logo stamped on them. My dad sewed them for me." He looked down at his pyjamas and then up. "My brothers have called me different names, but never Pyjama Boy, and I'm..."

"Enough! Why do you talk *so* much! You're making my head spin." The Billy Goat sat down on a flat rock, put on a pair of dark-rimmed glasses, and then crossed its front legs. "Joseph, Sprout, G.I. Joe—who cares? Just listen up, Pyjama Boy. When you least expect it, that crooked old man tall as a giant's rake will sneak up on you and eat you. He's very clever about it because he can't run very well anymore. He's so big and clumsy and old. But stay alert at all times when you're around Wilbur. I suggest you turn around this instant and go back where you came from." The Billy Goat shook its hoof at Joseph. "Understand me, Pyjama Boy?"

"Well, to be honest, no. I don't understand." Joseph turned and pointed to the mountains. "To answer your question, I think I came smashing and crashing into that fence, after zooming and zipping down a hillside, after swooshing and whooshing down a snow-covered peak, barrelling fast and faster down the mountain, dodging large boulders, sliding over frozen streams and under giant cedars, and ploughing through giant snow banks. The snow beneath me suddenly disappeared and I rolled like a barrel down a steep cliff, bumping and scraping along the ground, after floating and fluttering down a shaft filled with bright

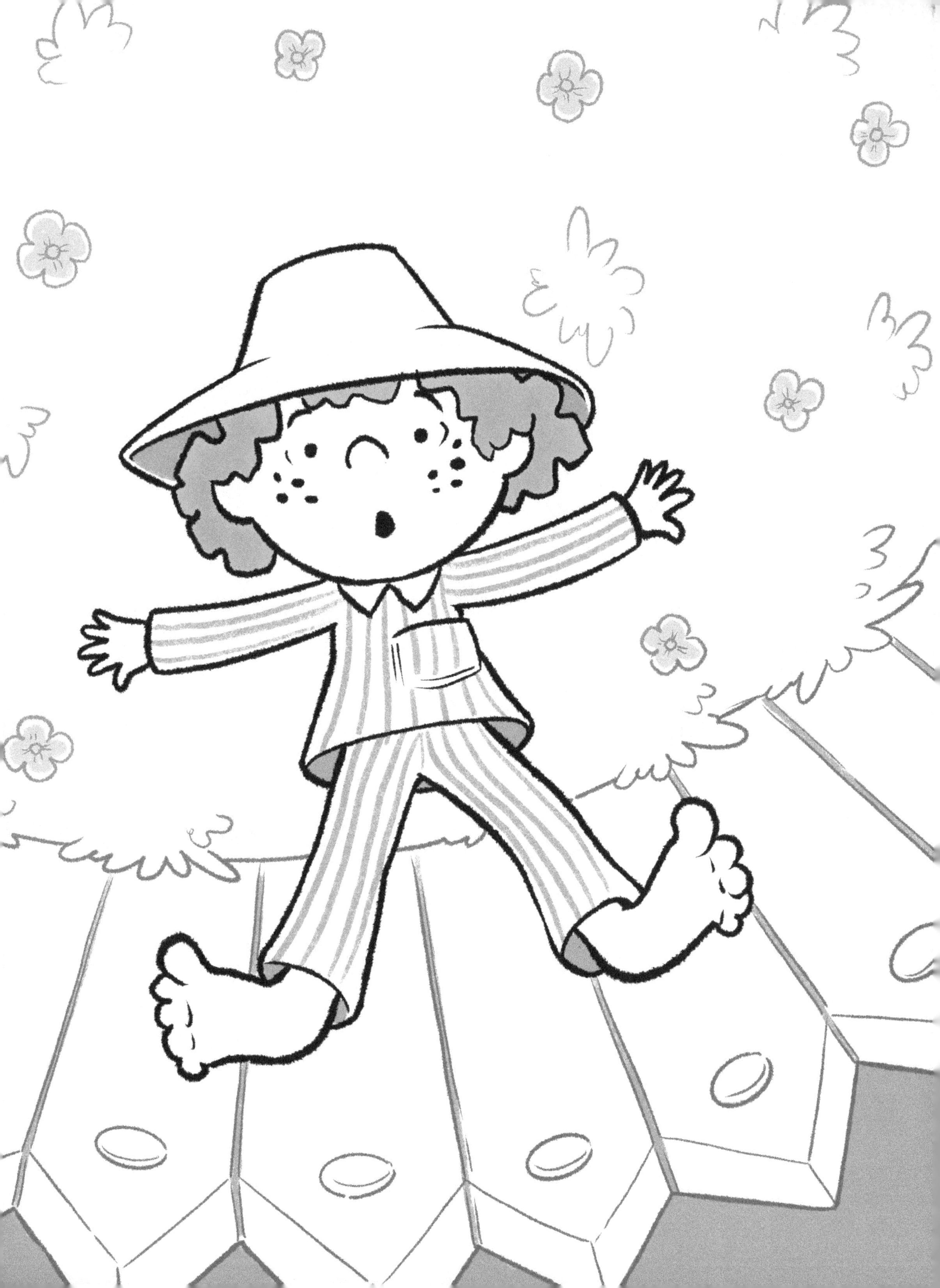

light, after bumping and banging down a dark tunnel, after thumping and thudding down a hole in Grandpa's magical cavern, after tumbling and fumbling into this crazy dream, after watching a falling star in the night sky and saying, 'Star light, star bright, the first star I see tonight; I wish I may, I wish I might, have the wish I wish tonight,' after plopping into bed, after gobbling garbanzo beans roasted in magical sand in Grandpa's fire pit."

"Stop! You talk too much."

The Billy Goat rose and pranced over to another fallen log. The Billy Goat butted its head in between talking. "To answer your question, my name is Buffy." *Butt!* "I live in the valley down below called Blackberry Bog." *Butt!* "I have so many kids I don't know what to do." *Butt!* "So I come to this hillside for some rest and relaxation." *Butt!* "I had more kids but Old Man Wilbur snuck up on them and ate them." *Butt!* "I don't want you or anyone else to get eaten by that crooked old man." *Butt!* "Wilbur has lived here in Zorak in that steeple for 343 years with his giant tomcat." *Butt!*

"Zorak?" Joseph whispered. "Is that where I am?"

The Billy Goat turned away from Joseph and bounded along the dirt road towards Blackberry Bog. Before disappearing around the first bend, he shouted, "Goodbye Joseph, Sprout, G.I. Joe, Pyjama Boy, and good luck getting back home. You best be careful. Don't get too close to old man Wilbur. I'm warning you."

Joseph sat down on a fallen log and wiggled his toes. "I'm not going to listen to a silly old Billy Goat! Whoever heard of a talking goat? That's ridiculous." He got to his feet and cautiously continued up the hillside towards the steeple, deeper and deeper in the land called Zorak.

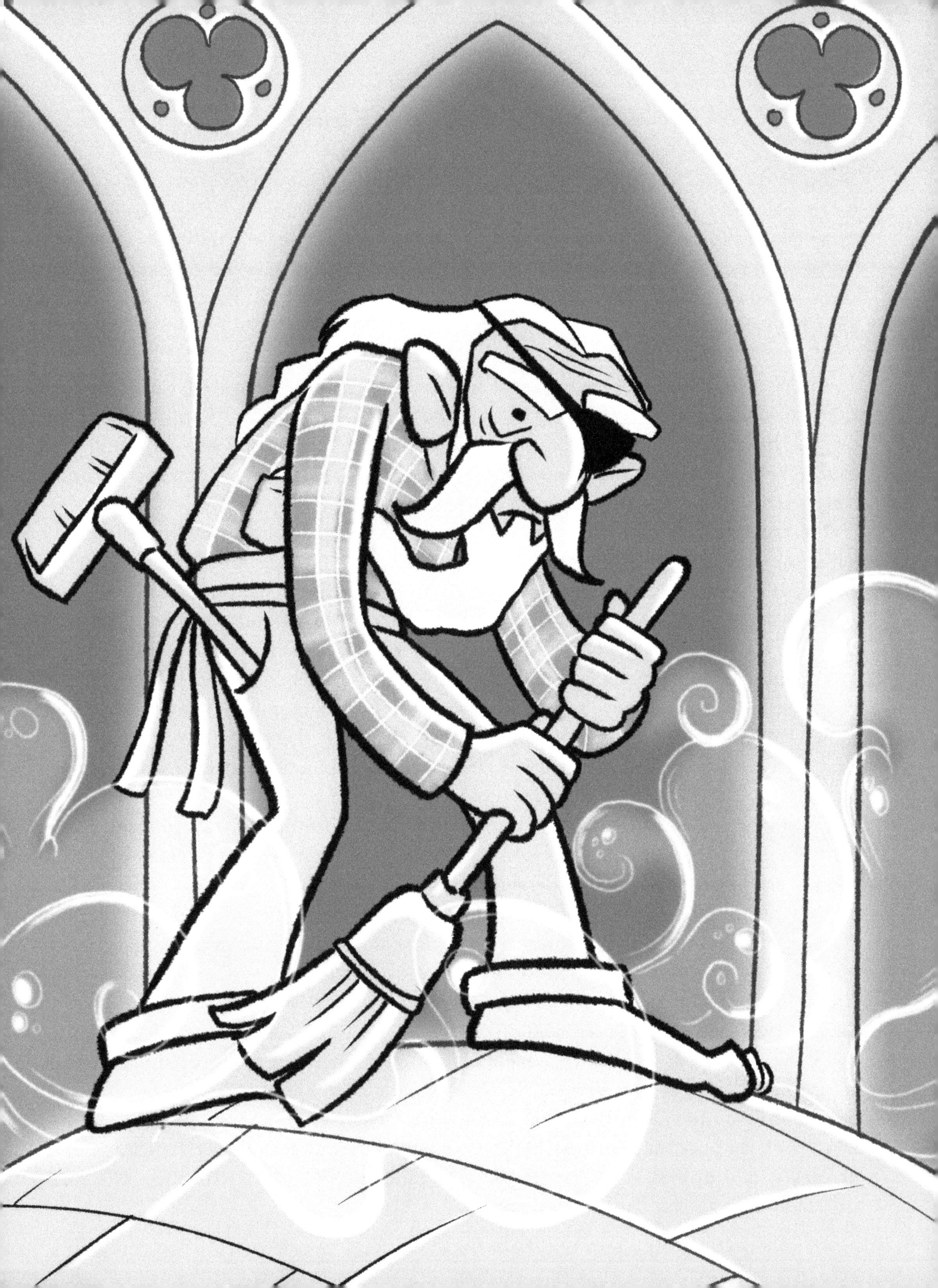

What Have We Here?

Joseph hid behind four large empty wooden crates piled high in a corner and watched a crooked old man tall as a giant's rake, with a long, triangular face, jug-like ears, prominent nose and a black patch over his left eye, sweeping the church steeple. He peered across the dimly lit room through wide slits and spotted a rickety rocking chair in the corner of the room, below a row of empty shelves. He discreetly looked over the crates.

"Oh my, what on earth is that?"

Joseph eyeballed the biggest, fattest, furriest cat he had ever seen, curled up next to a crackling potbellied stove in the opposite corner of the room. He placed his hand over his mouth to stifle any noise. The cat wore an orange and purple-striped tie and four different coloured sneakers—blue, green, yellow and red. A garland of garlic hung from wooden rafters above the cat.

The crooked old man's face looked like a worn-out old horse saddle—leathery, nut-brown and rugged. A corked jug of water and small barrel of wine squished and swashed in one of two enormous pockets of his over-sided, threadbare grey sweater. A butternut squash, small sack of chestnuts, and apples stuffed the other pocket. A dustpan wider than a breadbox hung from the crooked old man's back pocket. He swept the floorboards with a corn broom in his spade-like hands, and a thick cloud of dust rose from the floor up and around his bare feet and spindly legs. His braided, snow-white ponytail that dangled over his drooping left shoulder down past his dirty feet, swayed back and forth to the rhythm of his sweeping. A matching pointy beard was tucked in the front pocket of his plaid shirt.

"I wonder how many times he's tripped over that there beard," Joseph whispered. He folded his arms on top of the crate and rested his chin in his hands. "He must be Old Man Wilbur, and that curious little thing must be his pet cat."

He watched through the cloud of dust with a half-open eye, the crooked old man scowling and sweeping. Deep furrows ran across Wilbur's forehead above sunken cheeks. A tinkling sound interrupted the silence of the steeple. Wilbur leaned the corn broom against the door, knelt down, and sifted through the debris with his gnarled fingers. He fished a shiny gold coin off the floor.

"Well, well, well, what have we here, Acorn?" A whistling sound escaped through a large gap in his two rotten front teeth when he spoke, filtering through his thick and handlebar moustache. He stomped across the planked floor, opened a large wooden chest, and emptied the contents of his pockets, putting the butternut squash, sack of chestnuts, and apples into the chest, before placing the corked water jug and small barrel of wine on the floorboards.

"My heavens, those there are the biggest and deepest pockets I've ever seen." Joseph squatted down behind the crates and then sat cross-legged on the dusty floor staring at Wilbur's ragged green overalls hanging on his scraggy frame. "I can't wait to show Grandpa this place. I bet he's never been *here* before. This is *my* secret. Emma would love to see this!"

Wilbur plopped down onto his rickety rocking chair and put on his fedora. The crooked old man as tall as a giant's rake rolled the gold coin between his thumb and index finger. He bit down on the coin. "By golly Acorn, I think I've found money for our supper tonight." Acorn crawled over to the rocking chair, dragging the striped tie along the floor and leaving a trail in the dust. The giant cat rubbed her head against Wilbur's bare feet. The old man fished his hands inside his overalls and pulled out a clump of chewing tobacco and a jaw harp.

"Now this calls for a celebration, Acorn." He snorted and chuckled. "I've been saving this here piece of chewing tobacco for a rainy day." He wedged the tobacco between his cheek and his gum. "I reckon now's as good a time as any to savour it. Today's our lucky day, Acorn."

"Acorn? That's an odd name for a cat," Joseph whispered.

The crooked old man flipped the sparkling gold coin high in the air and it landed back down on his forearm. "I think I'll rest here for a spell, Acorn, and think 'bout this here coin." He lay back in his rickety rocking chair and pulled the massive fedora over his eyes. "So, whatcha think's the best thing to buy with this here coin, Acorn? And where do you think it came from?" He lifted the fedora and scratched his head. "It sure beats the heck out of me! I ain't seen one of these coins in a dog's age." Wilbur fell silent and then talked to himself. "I have a hankerin' for some salted herring, but herring only keeps for a few days. I reckon I can buy me a few loaves of bread, but bread is an awful waste because you lose all the crumbs. There's gotta be something else I can buy."

Wilbur scratched his nose and then plucked a long hair from his left nostril.

Joseph grimaced. "Now that there is a mighty, nasty, ill-mannered old man." Acorn scurried back to the burlap sack, curled up, and purred loudly. "That there sounds like no cat I've ever heard. She's louder than a field tractor and twice as big," Joseph chuckled.

Wilbur placed the jaw harp between his lips and strummed on the thin metal reed. Three high-pitched twangs vibrated amid the crackle and hissing of the wood-burning stove and the incessant purring of the tomcat. He paused to continue talking about food. "And if I buy me some nuts? Well, then I'll have to throw away the shells. Now that's an awful waste." He dropped the harp into the pocket of his sweater. "Maybe I won't buy anything right now! I reckon I have enough food for a few more days." As he rose and stomped over to a shelf on the opposite wall, the floorboards shook so much that Joseph held on to the rattling crates for dear life.

"Golly, that there's some mean stomping," Joseph said to himself. "I'll bet he's eaten a couple of kids today, and that's why he doesn't want to buy any food."

Wilbur slowly surveyed the contents on the shelf—a can of beans, two onions, and a half loaf of bread. He shook his head and grumbled in disapproval. "Heck, Acorn, me thinks I'll buy me a jug of fresh goat's milk for now and save the rest for a rainy day. Whatcha think? I still have me a butternut squash, some apples, and a sack of chestnuts in that there chest." He tapped his fedora firmly on his head. "Yes, that's what I think I'll do." Acorn's eyes lazily followed the old crooked man stomping to the door. She rolled onto her rotund belly and went back to sleep.

Tired of sitting on the hard, uneven floor, Joseph sprung to his feet and spotted three swallows wearing black top hats, white gloves, and yellow scarves perched on the windowsill.

"What on earth have we here? First a talking Billy Goat with glasses, then a tomcat wearing a striped tie and coloured sneakers, and now three birds dressed to go to some fancy show. Boy-oh-boy, do I ever have a story for bug-eyed Noah! He'll never believe it. Emma would love to see this!"

The swallows stared down at the sleeping tomcat and then at Wilbur opening the front door. An enormous umbrella was tucked under his arm.

"I'll be back in a jiffy with some fresh goat's milk, Acorn." The heavy wooden door shut behind Wilbur with a thud. Joseph tiptoed to the window and looked out at him loping along a dirt road that led deeper into Zorak. The three swallows gazed at the young boy with the blue eyes, removed their top hats, and bowed to Joseph.

"I'm Do," the middle swallow said. "This is my brother Re and that's my brother Mi. We're pleased to meet you, Sir Joseph, Joseph, and G.I. Joe."

Joseph stared at the speaking swallow with an astonished look on his face. "So, you're the boy with the three names who spoke to Buffy the Billy Goat two hours ago? Is that right, sir?"

"Are you for real?" asked Joseph, scratching his head.

"Sir, are you or are you not the boy who fell from the sky, slid down the mountain, and tumbled into our town?"

Startled, Joseph took a few steps back. "Grandpa will never believe me." He shook his head. "And *if* I am the boy who fell from the sky," Joseph responded, "then what?"

"Sir, we are here to ask if you are indeed the person who fell from the sky. If you are, did you happen to see Betsy the Cow?"

"Betsy... the Cow?"

"Yes sir. You know, Betsy, the one who jumped over the moon the evening China the Dish ran away with Scoop the Spoon?"

"You have got to be kidding me?"

"Well, sir, it's a very simple question—did you or did you not see Betsy the Cow?"

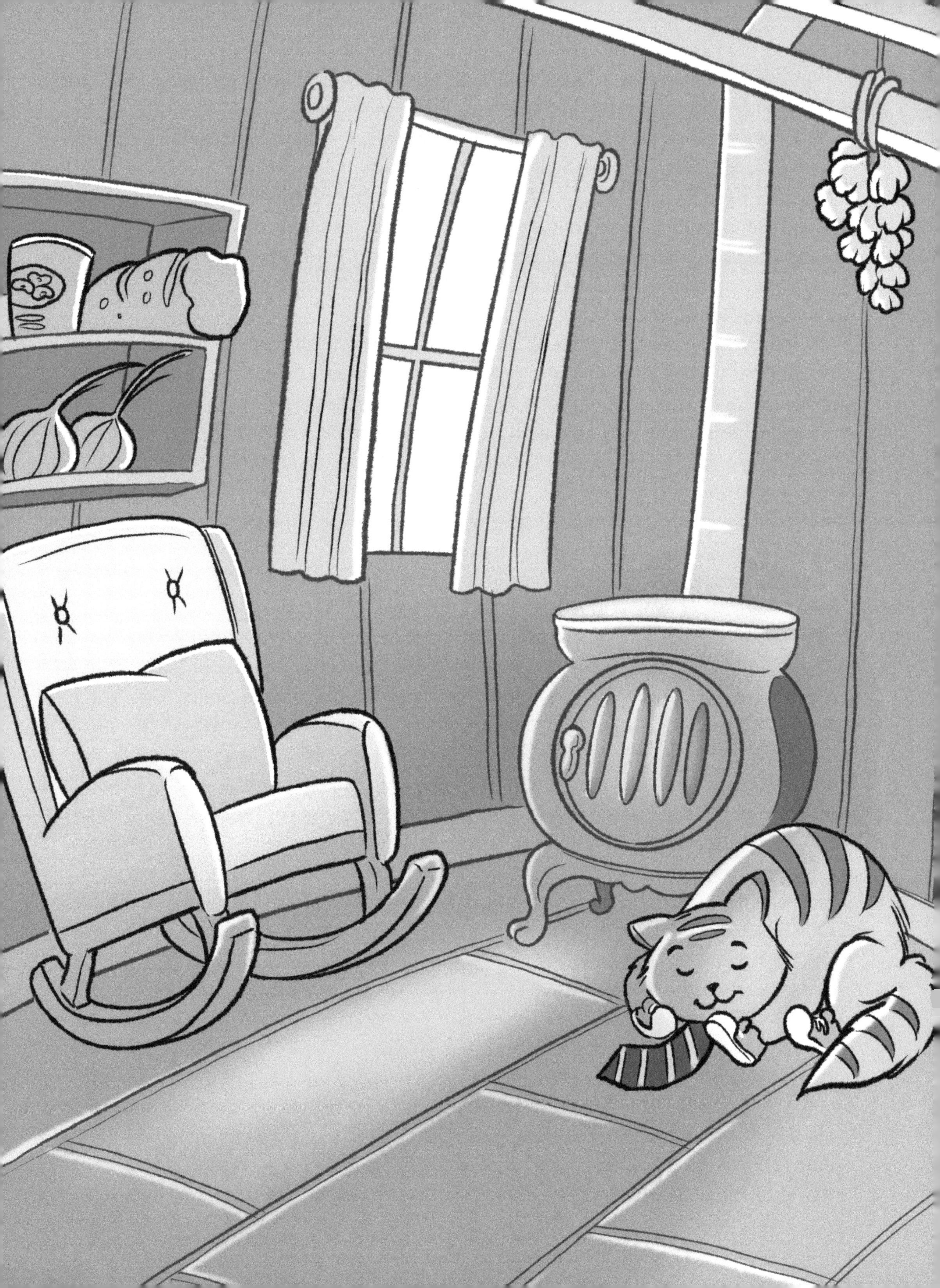

"You're telling me that a dish named China ran away with a spoon named Scoop, and then a cow named Betsy jumped over the moon?"

"Well answer their question, boy. It's rather simple—yes or no? They're not asking you to lasso the moon or something."

Joseph spun around and saw the voice belonged to the tomcat wearing the purple-and-orange striped tie and four different coloured sneakers. He looked stunned that a talking tomcat was scolding him for being slow in answering a question, a question asked by a talking swallow named Do dressed in a top hat, white gloves, and yellow scarf. "It's not possible!"

"Sir, there is no need to shout. A simple yes or no will suffice," Re chirped.

"I didn't see any cow or any dish or any spoon," Joseph finally answered, not sure of what he actually saw or thought he saw as he fell. "Can any of you help me get back home to Grandpa's Farm?" he asked, scratching his chin in disbelief.

"Kid, I saw you hiding behind those crates and I never told the crooked old man," Acorn responded in a sharp tone. "I saved your life. Wilbur would have had you as an appetizer if he had spotted you. I don't care one way or another whether he eats you. But don't you dare get upset with us, kid!"

"Everyone, please stop. My name is Joseph. I mean Sprout. Not Kid. Not Sir. Not Pyjama Boy.

"So which is it, Joseph or Sprout?" Acorn demanded. "You're confusing me."

"Please call me Joseph. Yes, Joseph would be fine. I'm ten years old and I live with my family on Grandpa's farm. I'm lost. I'm hungry. I want to go home. Can you help me? I don't know why I'm here or how I got here. I don't know what I'm doing speaking to swallows and a cat and a goat. I just want to go home."

"Sir, whatever you do, don't let Wilbur see you or you'll end up as his dinner," Mi warned, adjusting the yellow scarf around his neck. "Sir, if Wilbur sees you, I suggest you run as fast as you can! He can't catch you. He's a crooked old man. Just run and don't stop running!"

"Hide, hide!" Do flapped his wings and fluttered on the windowsill. "Wilbur's almost back home!"

Joseph scrambled back behind the wooden crates.

"Kid, just hide there and relax." Acorn curled up on the burlap sack by the potbellied stove. "Do, Re and Mi, nestle on the windowsill and start singing," instructed Acorn.

Old Man Wilbur entered the steeple carrying a large jug of goat's milk. He huffed and puffed and plucked another hair from his nostril. He stomped to the shelf and popped a butternut squash into his mouth, and then crunched and chewed and spit seeds into the open hearth. He placed the jug of goat's milk on the chest, filled a bowl with fresh milk and set it down beside Acorn. "This is for you, my faithful furry friend."

The crooked old man flopped onto his rickety rocking chair and retrieved the jaw harp from the enormous pocket of his grey sweater. He placed it between his teeth and strummed and twanged. Acorn and the three swallows plugged their ears. Three minutes later—after precisely thirty-three snores—Wilbur was sleeping like a baby.

Acorn rolled onto his side. Through an opening between the crates, Acorn spotted Joseph sound asleep on the hardwood floor with his arms tucked under his chin. Do, Re and Mi bowed and sang a beautiful lullaby on the windowsill overlooking the cluster of stone dwellings that leaned against each other like toppling dominoes.

There's a Mouse in the House

At three o'clock in the afternoon—as Joseph dozed behind the wooden crates and Old Man Wilbur slept like a log in his rickety rocking chair and Acorn snored like a field tractor on the burlap sack—a chubby dormouse swung leisurely on the garland of garlic hanging from a wooden rafter above the cat. The fury blue-grey mouse, with a long, thick snout, swung on the garland with one hand and held a cob pipe in the other hand. The singing sparrows had long since flown away.

"Is anyone around here ever going to wake up? Pip the Dormouse is starving." He stopped swinging and sat up on the garland of garlic, rubbed his growling tummy and licked his lips. "How about a chunk of cheese or a piece of bread? Wake up down there! Heck, it's the middle of the afternoon—wake up!"

Pip's cherry nose twitched and his two big, floppy pink ears drooped over his shoulders. "Hi-ho, hi-ho, it's off to *eat* I go."

Joseph opened his eyes, listened for a moment, and groggily got to his feet. He yawned and stretched and rubbed his bloodshot eyes. He squinted over the crates. His eyes flitted round the steeple and focused themselves slowly on the chubbiest, furriest mouse he'd ever seen. Its long pink tail, orange-coloured feet, and drooping belly swung back and forth above Acorn's head. Small puffs of smoke billowed out from under his whiskers.

"Hello there," Joseph said in a low voice careful not to awaken Wilbur and Acorn. "Are you really speaking and singing and smoking?" Joseph's voice startled the chubby dormouse. He teetered and tottered recklessly, regained his balance, and then steadied himself on the garland. "Oh, I'm sorry if I frightened you," said Joseph, still rubbing his eyes.

Pip, longing for some food, bore down on the little boy with curly hair the colour of carrots and deep blue eyes the colour of the sky. "Got any chunks of cheese or a few crumbs, Sleepy Head?"

Joseph's eyes open as wide as a skillet. "I wish bug-eyed Noah could see me now! He'd be so jealous," said Joseph to himself. "Are you really a talking mouse?"

The dormouse slapped his forehead and pointed to Joseph. "Are you really a talking Sleepy Head?"

"Shh!" Joseph pointed across the room to Wilbur and Acorn. "Don't wake them."

"Of course I'm a mouse! What do I look like, a hippopotamus? Now come on, let's get something to eat—I'm starving!"

"Oh, so am I! And I'm so tired."

The chubby mouse with the pink floppy ears and the cherry nose slapped his forehead again. "Okay, I'll start again. Pip the Dormouse, that's me, and you're

Sleepy Head. I'm pleased to meet you, and you're pleased to meet me. So, hello, howdy and all that stuff. Now listen—I'm starving! Get it? Famished! Do you understand? Like, what language do you speak?"

Joseph smiled up at the angry dormouse with the small orange feet and the thin pink tail.

"Are you laughing at me? I tell you I'm hungry and you laugh at me? Listen Sleepy Head, I've been trying to wake you up for hours and the only response I've been getting from you three sleepy heads has been some tossing and turning, and every once in a while that crooked old man puts his fingers in his nostrils and plucks out a long wiry nose hair and spits seeds across the room. Look Sleepy Head, are you going to help me find food or do I have to gnaw on this smelly garlic?" Pip looked over intently at the boy, hoping his urgency came across in his face.

"My name isn't Sleepy Head. Actually, my name is..." Joseph, but my family and friends call me Sprout, and some call me G.I. Joe on account of my khaki-coloured overalls with the army logo stamped on them. My dad sewed them for me." He looked down at his pyjamas and then up. "My brothers have called me different names, but never Sleepy Head."

"Okay, Sleepy Head. I get it. Hurray! Goody for you. Now let's find food, chow, nourishment—I need something in my tummy. If I had a hat, I'd eat it!"

"I once had a hat—a straw hat. It was my most favourite hat in the whole wide world. But I lost it on my way here."

"By the way, *where* is here?" Pip struck a match and relit his cob pipe.

"Why, are you lost too?" Joseph said.

"I've been on my own quite a while Sleepy Head," Pip replied, a gnawing hunger making his stomach rumble and grumble. "I lost my family a long time ago."

"What happened?"

"My father and I were on our way to join my mother who was visiting her mother—my grandmother—in some village. I don't know the name." Pip's cheeks turned beet red. "We had been walking for hours over hill and over dale, under stone bridges, across vast open fields, and up some pretty steep cliffs, and we finally reached some pretty dense brush. Pa warned me to stay close to him. But I decided to stop and rest for a second— just a split second. I was too embarrassed to tell Pa. Then I saw the mulberry bush. I was starving. I bent down and started eating the delicious berries. I guess I should have never stopped to eat because that was the last time I saw Pa."

Pip wiped a tear from his eye. "I wandered for days on end looking for Pa. I never found him or Ma. That was a long time ago. I've been on my own ever since. I'm as lost as you are, kid. I travel from village to village, always on the hunt for food. I could smell this garland of garlic from a mile away, and I followed the stench figuring if there's garlic, there must be food."

Pip took a puff of his cob pipe.

"Geez, I've never seen a mouse smoke a pipe!" Joseph said with a big smile on his face.

Pip blew a round ring of smoke and said, "So tell me, Sleepy Head, er, Joseph. Where the heck are we? And how did *you* get here? And who in the world is Buffy?"

Joseph sat down cross-legged on the dusty floor. "We're in Zorak. Down below us is Blackberry Bog—that's where Buffy the Billy Goat lives. We're in a steeple and that child-eating, crooked old man there is Wilbur. He's lived here for 343 years with his giant tomcat." Joseph pointed to the cat on the burlap sack. "That there is Acorn."

"So, Buffy's a Billy Goat and Acorn's that ugly-looking cat with the funny looking orange tie?"

"I think I'm lost Pip. I mean, I opened my eyes and there I was, against a fence in that meadow staring up at those mountains."

"Before you go running at the mouth again, I just want to let you know that you're not lost... you're here. And I'm really hungry, and that's really my tummy grumbling. So how did you get here Sleepy Head?"

"I don't know where to begin. I mean...I guess...I'll start from the fence way down below."

"Keep it short Sleepy Head." Pip rested against the garland and stared down at the little boy. "I need food soon, very soon."

"To answer your question, I think I came crashing and smashing into that fence, after zooming and zipping down a hillside, after swooshing and whooshing down a snow-covered peak, barrelling fast and faster down the mountain, dodging large boulders, sliding over frozen streams and under giant cedars, and ploughing through giant snow banks. The snow beneath me suddenly disappeared and I rolled like a barrel down a steep cliff, bumping and scraping along the ground, after floating and fluttering down a shaft filled with bright light, after bumping and banging down a dark tunnel, after thumping and thudding down a hole in Grandpa's magical cavern, after tumbling and fumbling into this crazy dream, after watching a falling star in the night sky and saying, 'Star light, star bright, the first star I see tonight; I wish I may, I wish I might, have the wish I wish tonight,' after plopping into bed, after gobbling garbanzo beans roasted in magical sand in Grandpa's fire pit."

Joseph breathed deeply, rubbed his eyes, and was about to continue his story when Pip interrupted him. "Golly gee! Stop!" He slapped his forehead once, twice, three times and then whistled. "Stop your talking, Sleepy Head. It's time to put some food into this grumbling tummy."

"Shh! Please don't wake Wilbur. If he sees me, he'll eat me and you'd be inside his tummy in one gulp."

Pip scuttled across the rafters to a rope. He slid down onto the windowsill, jumped over Acorn, and scurried across the dusty floor to stand in front of Joseph. He hopped up onto a crate. "So, where does that giant keep the food?" he asked, taking a puff on his cob pipe.

"Well, I don't really know, but I remember seeing Wilbur emptying his pockets into that there chest. But there's no use searching because I saw him lock the chest with that giant padlock, and the key is in his left pocket. It's no use trying to get that key because it's enormous and it weighs more than you and me together. On that there shelf though I did see a can of beans, two onions and a half loaf of bread."

"Relax kid. Do you always talk so much? You sound like a fiddle."

Pip turned and sized up the scene. He quickly realized it would be too dangerous to try to jump onto the shelf directly above Wilbur's rickety rocking chair. "Much too risky!"

He sat on the crate, rubbed his snout, and stroked his whiskers, and thought silently, never for a moment taking his eyes off Wilbur, who plucked another hair from his left nostril and coughed and spit a butternut squash seed clear across the room.

"What's that?" Pip pointed to a large jug.

"Goat's milk and you had better stay away from it!" warned a baritone voice from across the room. "If Old Man Wilbur sees you, there's no telling what will happen."

Pip and Joseph stared at each other, afraid to look. They slowly turned their heads and saw a black-and-white checkered lizard resting on a ledge just above the door.

"What's wrong? It looks like you just a ghost."

"Where did you come from?" Joseph said.

"I'm Larry, the only checkered lizard in all of Zorak."

"That's strange! I've been in this here room for hours and I never noticed you before." Joseph scratched his head and said, "I wish Emma was here. She'd love to see this!"

"Well, I've been watching and listening to you two fools for the past hour. And I can guarantee, as much as I can guarantee that the sun rises in the east every morning, you're aiming to get into a heap of trouble if you mess with Old Man Wilbur. Take it from me. I've been around this here steeple since Moby Dick was a minnow." Larry the Lizard rolled on his back and chuckled. "I wouldn't even think about getting close to that jug of goat's milk. The last person who tried to steal from Wilbur… well, let's just say that his bones were ground into flour and then that flour was used to make bread. Boy, you two sure are dumb!"

Pip turned and gaped at the half-loaf of mouldy bread on the shelf. "Yuk, bread made out of bones? No thanks. I'd rather kiss a toilet seat." He rubbed his drooping, grumbling belly and gazed back at the jug of goat's milk.

Larry got to his feet and shook his head. "If brains were leather, you two wouldn't have enough to saddle a June bug."

Pip leapt onto Joseph's shoulder. "Hey buddy, what do you think? Forget about that there miserable lizard. I think he's about as useful as a pogo stick in quicksand."

"Why did I eat so many garbanzo beans, why?" Joseph said, ignoring Pip.

"But I thought you said you were hungry?"

"I am!" Joseph smacked his lips and rubbed his tummy.

"But you just said you wished you hadn't eaten all those garbanzo beans."

"Yes, but that was at Grandpa's farm... a long time ago."

Pip looked back to the jug of goat's milk.

"I'm warning you two, don't do it," Larry said. "Jeepers, you two sure are dumb if you actually think you can steal from Wilbur. You're just looking for a mess of trouble!" He scurried to the open window and jumped out.

"Hey Sleepy Head, so what do we do? Listen to a miserable, crazy checkered lizard and stand here like two dummies and starve, or go get us some grub?"

"I think I just lost my appetite," Joseph replied. "But if you really want some of that goat's milk, I think there is a way to get it."

Pip rubbed his snout against Joseph's cheek and said, "I need just a little sip... just a wee drop. Please tell me how to get some... pretty please... pretty please with sugar on top."

"Well, I guess I could, but I don't want to be responsible for what might happen." "Aw, don't worry. What could possibly happen?"

"Well, I do remember one of the three swallows—I think it was Mi—said that if you run as fast as you can, Wilbur won't be able to catch you because he's a crooked old man."

"Perfect." Pip smiled. "That's exactly what I'll do then."

"But don't stop running, understand?"

"I'll run faster than a runaway train, that's for sure."

"I think you better run faster than that."

"Are you coming, Sleepy Head, or we're just going to stand here and wait until Old Man Wilbur finds us and eats us?"

"Do worms have armpits?" Joseph grinned and Pip giggled. The dormouse whispered into Joseph's ear, "Don't you worry kid. I can do this. I may be as nervous as a long-tailed cat in a room full of rocking chairs, but I'm so rumbly in my tummy right now that I could eat an ox! Here goes nothing, Sleepy Head."

Pip scurried down Joseph's striped pyjamas and onto the floorboards. He raised his snout, sniffed the air, and zeroed in on his target. The jug of goat's milk smelled delicious and inviting. Pip's pencil-thin pink tail curled up into a knot, his floppy ears perked straight up above his head, and his nose twitched. He took a deep breath and gaped as he looked up at Joseph. "I could use two of Acorn's running shoes right about now." He winked. "Wish me luck, Sleepy Head. I'm gonna need it."

Joseph shut his eyes and crossed his fingers. "Good luck, Pip," he murmured.

The chubby dormouse dashed across the dusty floor, jumped over the purring tomcat with the striped tie and four different coloured sneakers, climbed up the rope, scurried across the rafters to the other side of the room, slid down another rope, and then leapt onto the wooden chest beside Old Man Wilbur and slammed into the side of the open jug as his overanxious mouth reached for the lip. Milk spilled onto the chest. Pip slurped the warm milk, burped, glanced around the room, and slurped some more. His movement rattled the iron padlock on the chest. Wilbur snarled and snorted awake in his rickety chair. The rocking chair screeched and the jaw harp clattered to the floor. He flung the fedora from his face and the hat hit the shelf with the can of beans, two onions, and half-loaf of mouldy bread. They toppled to the floor. The steeple shook and quaked and the bells in the belfry clanged for the first time in 343 years.

"What? Who's there?" Wilbur grumbled as he got to his feet. "Who dares interrupt my sleep?"

"Look out Pip, here he comes!" squeaked Mi, who had returned and sat perched on the windowsill.

Wilbur lunged for Pip sitting on the wooden chest with the milk moustache. Pip froze in his tracks. His squinty pink eyes appeared to grow larger than the giant's saucer. Pip stared at Wilbur, then at Joseph.

"Run as fast as you can!" Mi shouted. "He won't catch you; he's a crooked old man."

"Who dares to interrupt my sleep? Who dares to enter my steeple without permission? I'll eat anyone I see!" Wilbur licked and smacked his lips.

"I can't watch. I can't!" Do cried out as he landed beside Mi on the windowsill. He shut his eyes and buried his beak under his wing.

Wilbur turned and faced Do on the windowsill. He grinned. "I'll have you for a snack, my little feathered friends—later tonight! For now, I have me a mouse to catch. I hate visitors!"

Joseph closed his eyes, slapped his cheeks, and pinched his nose. "Wake up! It's only a dream!" He opened his eyes, hoping to wake up in his soft, warm bed, and saw Pip in Wilbur's grip. Pip popped out of Wilbur's grasp and darted up to the highest rafter in the steeple.

He stared down, way down, at the pencil-thin pink tail dangling between Wilbur's finger and thumb. "Oh my, oh my!" Pip squeaked.

Panting after the run, he glanced at his behind with only one eye opened to where his tail used to be. "Oh my, Wilbur's got my tail! Someone help me! Wilbur's got my tail!"

Butt! The steeple door thundered open. Buffy the Billy Goat came crashing in, followed by Larry the Lizard. Wilbur turned towards the open door, holding Pip's tail up in the air, huffing and puffing.

"Give it back, Wilbur," Buffy pleaded. "Give the mouse back his tail, and then he and the boy will leave and never return!"

"The boy? What boy?" Wilbur snarled. "I love eating little boys!" He scanned the steeple and spotted Joseph behind the pile of crates standing on trembling legs.

"Come on, Wilbur," Buffy said. "Give the mouse back his tail and he and the boy will leave and never ever return."

"And what about my goat's milk?" The crooked old man turned this way and that way, ogling the young boy, peering at the Billy Goat, staring at the lizard, gazing at the swallows on the windowsill, and gawping at the pencil-thin pink tail dangling in his right hand. He turned back to Joseph.

"Give the mouse his tail Wilbur," tweeted Do and Mi. "Then they'll leave and never ever disturb you again."

"I'll eat you three as appetizers first, and then I'll eat that lizard, then that there goat, and finally that scrawny little boy for dessert!" roared Wilbur. "And then if I'm still hungry, I'll eat that lazy-good-for-nothing tomcat!"

Acorn peeped out from under the burlap sack, stared at the antics in the steeple, and then cowered under the burlap sack in silence.

"Never will I return that rodent his tail—never!" Wilbur boomed and stomped his bare feet against the floorboards. The boards cracked and popped and the steeple suddenly rumbled, sending the crates toppling to the ground and leaving Joseph with nowhere to hide.

Wilbur huffed and puffed and lifted the half-empty jug of milk up off the floor.

"Where's my goat's milk?"

"Please, sir," Joseph murmured. "If you give my friend Pip back his tail, I will see to it that we replace the goat's milk Pip spilled and we'll never ever disturb you again—ever—promise."

The Tale of the Missing Tail

Old Man Wilbur peered down at Joseph with the half-empty milk jug in one hand and the pencil-thin pink tail in the other. "And how *long* have you been snooping around in my home you…you morsel? How long? I've already heard about your crazy journey, so save your breath, boy. How long you…you morsel?" Joseph cowered before the crooked old man tall as a giant's rake, with a long triangular face, jug-like ears, prominent nose and patch over his left eye. Before he could respond, Wilbur emptied the remaining goat's milk down his gullet and tossed the empty glass jug across the room. It smashed against the wall and shattered into a million pieces. Wilbur spluttered and stomped. The steeple shook and quaked.

Joseph looked up at the old man.

"My name isn't Morsel. Actually, my name is…" Joseph stepped out from behind the toppled crates. He looked up, way up, astounded at how tall and how crooked the old man stood.

Wilbur plucked a wiry hair from his nostril and spit a seed clear across the room and out the window. "For a morsel of a boy, you sure have a lot to say Morsel!"

"Please sir, I mean Wilbur, I mean Sir Wilbur, if you give Pip back his tail, I'll see to it that we replace the goat's milk Pip spilled and we'll never ever disturb you again."

"How and where are you going to get me my goat's milk?" Wilbur chortled and stuck his thumb into his ear, wiggled out a big glob of wax, and plopped it into his mouth. Pip shielded his eyes and shook his head. Larry the Lizard turned to Buffy. "Wow, this boy's dumber than a bag of nails!" He crawled onto Buffy's back. "Let's get out of here."

Buffy butted his head once, twice, three times against the wooden floorboards, and then trotted out of the steeple through the broken-down door and down the winding path to Blackberry Bog. Do, Re and Mi fluttered away. Wilbur sat back down in his rocking chair and picked up the jaw harp. He felt all his 343 years and didn't have the energy to chase the boy and dormouse. 'Later,' he thought, 'I'll pounce on them when they least suspect it, and I won't have to do any running after them.'

"You and your tail-less mouse have exactly three hours to get me my milk. If by sundown I don't have a full jug of fresh goat's milk, then you can forget about getting back this disgusting tail!" Wilbur leaned forward and scowled. "At sundown, you'll both be invited to dine with me. We'll be having roasted dormouse and boy stew."

"Come on, Virgil! We have to find us some fresh goat's milk so I can get my tail back," Pip said.

Joseph looked around the room. "Did you just call me Virgil? Nobody's ever called me Virgil before. My name is Joseph, but my family and friends call me Sprout and some call me G.I. Joe on account of my khaki-coloured overalls with the army logo stamped on them. My dad sewed them for me." Joseph looked down at his striped pyjamas and then, back up at Pip. My brothers have called me different names, but never..."

"Yes, yes I know," Pip interrupted. "Your name isn't Virgil. Old Man Wilbur recently called you Morsel, Acorn called you Kid, Do, Re and Mi called you Sir Joseph, and Buffy the Billy Goat called you Pyjama Boy. Pip—that's me, the chubby and now tail-less dormouse that smokes a cob pipe like your Pa—called you Sleepy Head. Larry the Lizard called you Dumb for entering this steeple. Your best friend Noah called you Stupid Head, but never Virgil. Your grandpa once called you Tadpole. All right, all right—I've heard it already! I'm calling you Sprout from now on. Yes, Sprout—Sprout's perfect."

Pip remained safely atop the highest rafter in the steeple and looked at his rump where his pencil-thin pink tail used to be. He scurried down to Joseph and handed him his cob pipe for safekeeping. Joseph stuffed it into his pyjama pocket.

"Let's get cracking and catch up to Buffy and that mean lizard," Pip shouted. "Buffy said he lives in Blackberry Bog. He'll know where to find goat's milk—he's a goat."

And so began a series of incredible encounters as they trudged through Zorak hoping to get to Blackberry Bog in search of Buffy the Billy Goat.

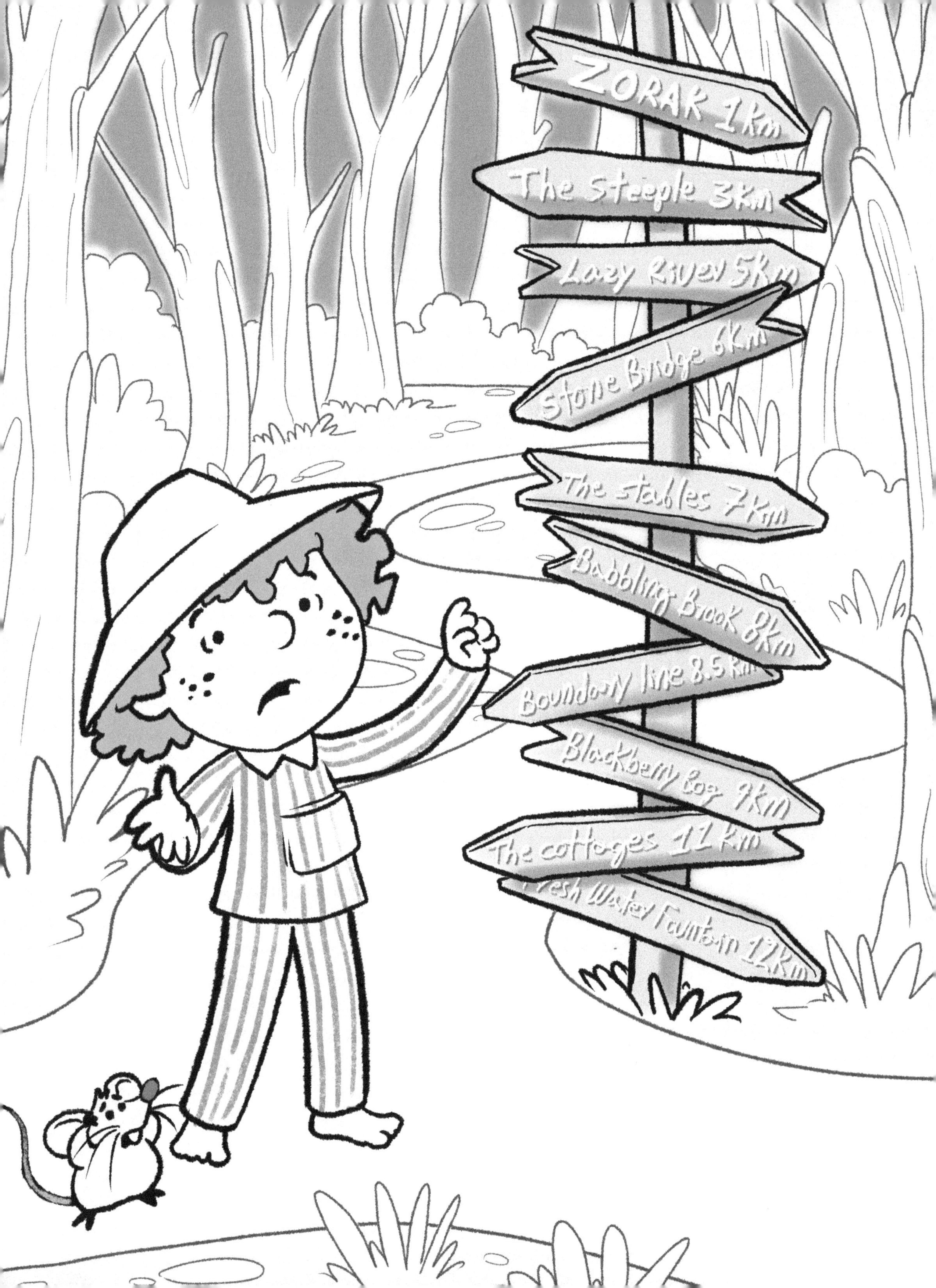
ZORAK 1km
The Steeple 3km
Lazy Rivev 5Km
Stone Bridge 6Km
The stables 7Km
Babbling Brook 8Km
Boundary line 8.5 Km
Blackberry Bog 9Km
The cottages 11 Km
resh Water Fountain 12Km

Whistling a Merry Tune

Pip curled up in the front pocket of Joseph's striped pyjama top as the pair trudged down the hillside.

"It sure is a beautiful day," Joseph said, stopping to look up into the bright blue sky. Pip poked his head out, sniffed the warm, fragrant air, and sneezed once, twice, three times. His eyes watered. His nose twitched.

"We must be near a lemon orchard Sprout. I remember journeying through this orchard to get to the steeple and I almost sneezed my snout right off my face."

"You would be one funny looking dormouse without a snout!"

"You mean without a snout *and* a without a tail." Pip nosedived back into Joseph's pyjama pocket and stuck out his tail-less chubby behind. He sneezed again and tumbled, rump and all, to the bottom of Joseph's pocket. They both broke out into laughter.

"Hey Pip, Grandpa always told me that when the sun touches the treetops, then there are three more hours of daylight." Joseph pointed up at the blazing sun in the distance. His eyes widened and his jaw dropped when he spotted a tiny ladybug holding a polka-dotted umbrella hovering overhead in the gentle breeze whistling a merry tune. She wore patent leather shoes with shiny golden buckles.

"Well good afternoon, young man. My, what beautiful blue eyes you have… *absolutely!*" She pointed to Pip with her umbrella. "And oh, what magnificent floppy pink ears… *absolutely!*" The ladybug looked back to Joseph and fluttered her eyelids. "My name is Lady Matilda. What's yours?"

Before answering, Joseph muttered, "Emma would love to see this!" Then he stared at the ladybug and said, "Actually, my name is…"

Pip quickly scurried onto Joseph's shoulder and slapped his hand across Joseph's mouth.

"Good morning, Lady Matilda. He's Sprout—that's what I call this little boy, and I'm Pip. We're on our way to Blackberry Bog to look for Buffy the Billy Goat. We need a jug of goat's milk for the crooked old man who lives way up there in that steeple so that I can have my tail back. If by sundown the jug is not full of fresh goat's milk, then I can forget about getting back my pencil-thin pink tail!" Pip's voice trembled. "At sundown, we'll all be invited to dine with Wilbur and on the menu is us—roasted dormouse and boy stew."

"If we don't replace the milk, Pip won't get back his tail, and I won't make it back home to Grandpa's farm," Joseph added.

"Oh! How *absolutely* frightful, *absolutely* horrendous, *absolutely* awful, *absolutely* dreadful, *absolutely* appalling, *absolutely* unspeakable!" Lady Matilda stomped her umbrella in the air. "I've already heard about your crazy journey down the mountain and smashing into the fence. Wow! *Absolutely* amazing!"

"My friend here still thinks he's in a dream," Pip piped in, "even though he spoke with Buffy the Billy Goat with a long white beard and the dark-rimmed glasses, even though he reasoned with Do, Re and Mi, the singing swallows who wear top hats, white gloves and yellow scarves, even though he was warned by Acorn, Wilbur's pet tomcat who wears an orange and purple-striped tie and four different coloured sneakers, even though he was scolded by Larry the black-and-white checkered lizard, and even though he's being accompanied by a pipe-smoking talking dormouse—that's me—and even as he speaks to you, Lady Matilda, a singing ladybug holding a polka dotted umbrella wearing patent leather shoes with shiny golden buckles."

"Oh, my!" Lady Matilda responded. "What an *absolutely* adventurous life you've led Sprout."

"Life! What life? All this has happened in the last few hours! And if we don't hurry up, we'll be tonight's dinner!"

"Oh, what an *absolutely* heroic tale. I must hurry home to tell the others…*absolutely!*" Lady Matilda's polka-dotted umbrella opened and she launched off Joseph's shoulder. An updraft caught the umbrella and catapulted the singing ladybug up into the heavens. "Goodbye, and continue to be strong and courageous." Her voice started to fade. "I *absolutely* hope you find a jug of goat's milk in Blackberry Bog. I *absolutely* hope that mean crooked old man gives you back your tail. Just follow the trail down into the valley and be *absolutely* sure to cross over to the other side of Lazy River."

Joseph marched across the meadow through the tall green grass with Pip nestled in his front pyjama pocket. "Hurry, Sprout! We don't want to be late crossing Lazy River or we'll never find our way to Blackberry Bog!"

Which Way to the River?

Tall maple trees lined the trail that wound down the hillside and into the valley. Many babbling brooks and flowing streams crisscrossed the valley floor. After a fast-paced trot down the rugged hillside, Joseph stopped and rested against a large boulder. The trail in front of him forked in two directions. He peered into his pyjama pocket.

"Hey Pip, I'm not sure which way to go. Which way do we go to get to the river?" Joseph wiped his forehead with his pyjama sleeve. He closed his eyes, pinched his nose, and then slapped his cheeks. "Wake up!" he shouted.

"Hey, stop saying that. This is not a dream." Pip stuck his head out of Joseph's pocket, hopped onto his shoulder, and turned Joseph's head to face him. "What's the meaning of this? Why would you want to leave me all alone in this here valley? Are you or are you not my friend? Will you or will you not help get back my tail?"

"I'm sorry, Pip. Of course I'll help you get back your tail."

Joseph jumped up and trudged over to a large blackberry bush. He picked some berries, plopped a few into his mouth, and handed a large, juicy blackberry to Pip. The tail-less dormouse tossed it up in the air and swallowed the berry when it fell into his open mouth. "Mmm, that tastes good!" Pip said, rubbing his tummy. "Okay, then we're in this together, through thick and thin?"

"*Absolutely!*" Joseph whistled. "It's Joseph and Pip right to the end!"

"You mean Sprout and Pip. And after we get back my tail, we'll find a way to your grandpa's farm."

"That's a deal—*absolutely!*"

Pip shook Joseph's hand. "Okay, get me another blackberry, partner."

"Your name should be 'Pit' as in 'bottomless pit,'" Joseph chuckled.

The two friends filled their tummies with more blackberries, enjoying the sweet juices of the plump fruit. Pip stopped chewing, pointing to a mound of dirt moving in front of Joseph. "Look, the earth is moving! The earth is moving! Be careful!"

Joseph froze and focused his attention on a giant tortoise emerging from the heap.

"What are you two staring at? Haven't you ever seen a tortoise taking a mud bath before?" The tortoise methodically knocked its shell against a boulder, shaking off excess mud. "Where are you two going? And why are your lips all purple?"

"Hello, Mr. Tortoise," Pip responded first. "My name is Pip and this is my friend and partner, Sprout."

"We've been eating blackberries," said Joseph, licking at the sides of his mouth. He sat down and leaned against the boulder and listened to a tail-less, chubby dormouse introducing himself to a talking tortoise wearing a scuba mask and snorkel, thinking "Emma would love to see this!"

"How do you do?" Pip said.

"Very well, Pit."

Joseph broke out in laughter when he heard the tortoise mistake Pip's name.

"I've been soothing my old bones under some hot mud. It does wonders, you know. I've been taking mud baths for over 600 years, on the second day of each month. I love mud baths!"

"It must be working because you don't look a day over 400!" Pip winked at Sprout. "And the name's Pip, not Pit, sir."

"There's no need to call me sir. My name is Thomas. Friends call me Tommy."

Joseph shook his head in disbelief. "I can't believe I'm listening to a 600-year-old talking tortoise wearing a scuba mask! I wish that bug-eyed Noah could see me now. He'd be so jealous."

Tommy the Tortoise stood on his hind legs and waddled over to Joseph, pointing a finger in his face.

"So, you think wearing a scuba mask is funny, do you? I don't want to irritate my eyes, so I wear this mask. Seeing as I do need to breathe while covered in mud, and so that I can hear, I use the snorkel. It's that simple. You should respect your elders. Let me tell you something, I'm as real as you and your chubby friend here, and you can ask anyone you want and they'll tell you my age. Now stop mumbling under your breath. Don't you know tortoises can hear everything?"

"I'm sorry if I have offended you sir," Joseph responded. "I'm just trying to find my way back home. But first I have to help my friend Pip get his tail back from the crooked old man who lives in the steeple at the top of the hill. I have to do it all before sundown, otherwise Wilbur—that's the crooked old man—is going to eat us for supper." Joseph stared up into the fading blue sky. "We're looking for Buffy the Billy Goat with a long white beard and the dark-rimmed glasses who lives in Blackberry Bog. We want to ask him for goat's milk to bring back to Wilbur. Wilbur said if we give him a jug of goat's milk he'll give Pip back his tail."

Tommy's head rose up slowly, his enormous shell swaying left and right, and tottered on his short, wrinkly legs. He looked up at the little boy with curly carrot-coloured hair that sprung out from under his straw hat.

"Oh, him! Everybody knows Wilbur loves eating little boys for breakfast, little girls for lunch, and anyone he can find for dinner. You best be careful." He pointed his scaly finger. "When you reach the edge of Lazy River, just beyond the stone bridge, ask for Allie the Alligator. She will take you safely across the river. Tell Allie that Tommy the Tortoise sent you and she'll take good care of you. Once you get across, you'll have to ask for directions to get to Blackberry Bog."

Pip dashed out of the Joseph's pyjama pocket and scurried to meet up with Tommy waddling away on the dirt path. He shook hands with the 600-year-old tortoise.

"Thank you so much for all your assistance. Now we must hurry. We need to get back to Wilbur before sunset with the goat's milk. I want my tail back!"

"One more thing before you go," Tommy said. "Is it true what everyone is saying about your friend sliding down the mountain and crashing into a fence?"

Pip scurried up Joseph's pyjamas and nosedived into the front pocket. "Yes... yes it's true. Please don't ask him to recount his journey. I can't bear to listen to it again... please."

"Don't you worry, Pip. I've already heard it. It really is an unbelievable journey." Tommy began to lumber his way under a thicket. "Goodbye then, and good luck, Sprout—I mean Joseph. I hope you find you way back home, and I hope your chubby friend gets back his tail. Remember to stay on the path to your right."

Pip poked his head out of the front pyjama pocket. "Where did the old tortoise go? I guess he's gone? "Let's get moving! It's getting late!" Pip scurried onto Joseph's shoulder and they followed the path on their right that wound through the valley.

"Hey Pip, I guess you didn't hear old Tommy the Tortoise wishing us luck. He hopes you get your tail back and I find my way back home."

"So do I, Sprout. So do I."

They continued their trek along the path searching for the stone bridge, the edge of Lazy River, and an alligator named Allie.

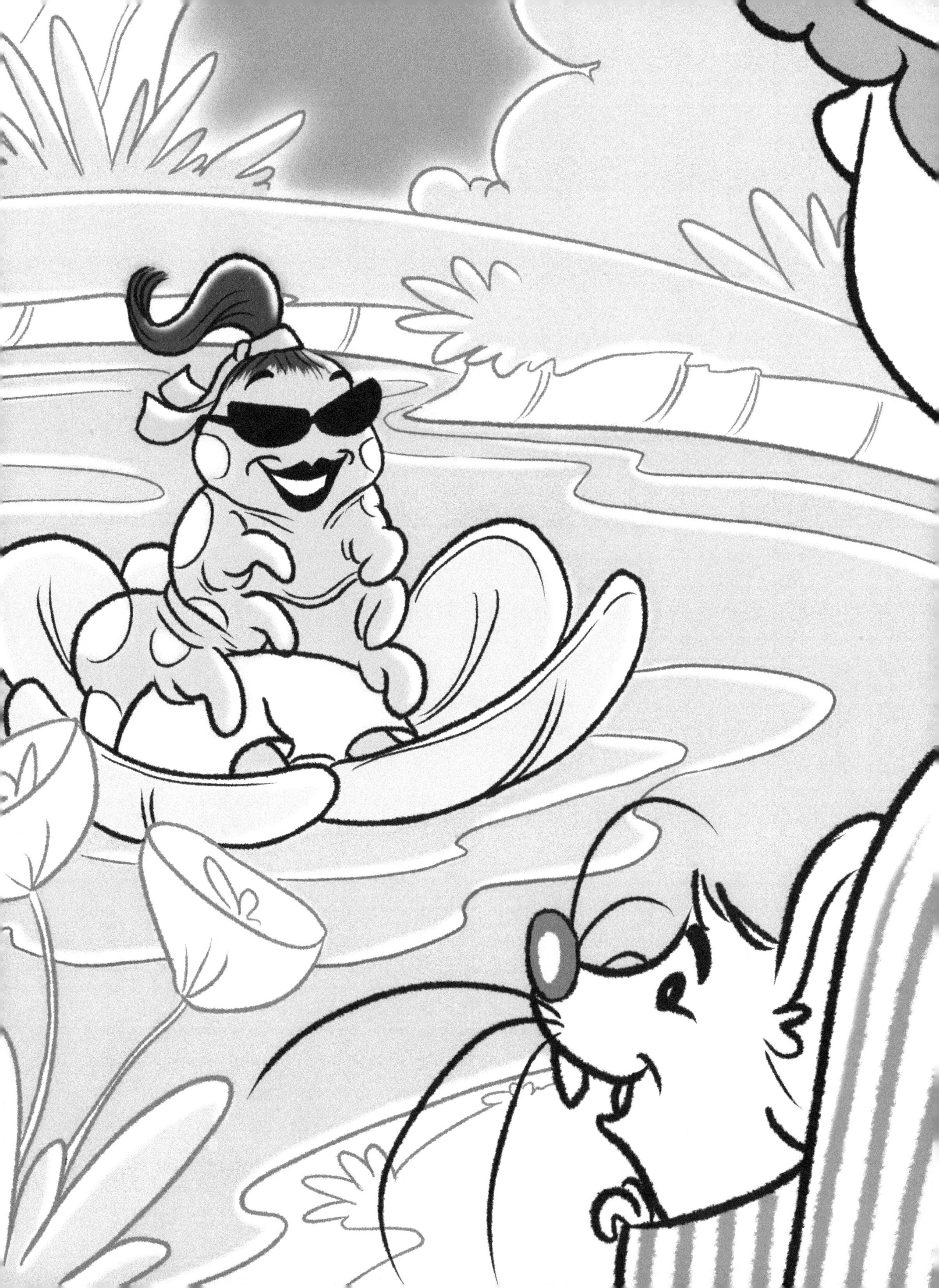

Frazzled

Mist blanketed the valley. A magnificent waterfall on their left plunged down into a pool of crystal clear water. Joseph and Pip trudged off the path towards the lake. Tall bulrushes and cattails lined the bank. Joseph peered through the tall reeds and spotted a boat made of tulip petals floating calmly on the lake.

"Wow, Pip! You'll never believe this, never!"

Pip scurried up to Joseph's shoulder and then hopped on top of his head to get a better look.

"Sprout, there's someone in a boat! I can see someone wearing a pair of green swim trunks and dark sunglasses. I think it's a girl. She has a pretty pink ribbon tied around her hair and she's rubbing something on... her orange body?"

"How can a girl have an orange body, Pip? Be serious."

"I am serious." Pip hopped up and down excitedly on Joseph's head. "She's heading towards us."

The water cradled the delicate boat as a gentle breeze pushed it towards land.

"I can see her, Sprout! She's... orange. She has pitch-black eyes and long beautiful eyelashes. Stand still, Sprout! She has a long body and two, four, six, eight, ten—ten feet. Ten tiny black feet."

"Oh please, Pip, stop rambling! Are you daydreaming?" Joseph peered through the reeds. He moved a little to his left, a little to his right. He moved back four steps and then forward three steps. Pip wildly held onto Joseph's locks, trying to maintain his balance on Joseph's head.

"She has a beautiful smile and plump, rosy cheeks, Sprout. She's rubbing tanning oil all over her long orange body. She's beautiful. She's coming this way. Sprout, are you listening? She's beautiful, and she's... a caterpillar? Yes, she's a caterpillar, and she's floating towards us. Here she is, Sprout... right in front of us."

Pip stared at the rosy-cheeked caterpillar with the lovely long eyelashes. He hopped off Joseph's head and onto his shoulder and then scampered into his front pyjama pocket.

"Speak to her, Sprout," Pip said, his eyes peeping out of Joseph's pocket. The orange caterpillar took off her sunglasses, adjusted her pink ribbon, and slunk onto shore. She extended her hand to Joseph.

"How do you do, young fella? I'm pleased to make your acquaintance. My name is Caroline."

"She's beautiful," Pip whispered.

"Excuse me, did you say something?" Caroline said.

"No, no…just hello."

Joseph reached for Caroline's extended hand when Pip noisily jumped onto his shoulder and startled the caterpillar. Pip took her hand in his before Joseph could.

"Good afternoon, Caroline. My name is Pip. We're on our way to Blackberry Bog to speak with Buffy the Billy Goat. We need goat's milk to take to the crooked old man who lives in the steeple in Zorak. He said if we give him a jug of goat's milk, he will give me back my tail. If by sundown the jug is not full of fresh milk, then I can forget about getting back my pencil-thin pink tail!" Pip's voice trembled, his cheeks turned beet red and his nose began to twitch. "At sundown, we'll all be invited to dine with Wilbur and on the menu is us—roasted dormouse and boy stew."

"Oh my, I think I'm going to faint," gasped Caroline the Caterpillar, curling up on top of a fallen log under the cool shade. She plucked a laced handkerchief out of her pocket and wiped drops of sweat from her brow. "I must have been in the sunshine for far too long."

"Are you alright?" asked Sprout.

"Yes, I'll be fine." She waved the laced handkerchief in front of her face. "Far too much sunshine, I suppose. So, you're Pip?"

"No, he's Pip." Joseph pointed to the tail-less, chubby dormouse.

"You must be Wilbur then, the chef who's cooking tonight's dinner?"

"My name isn't Wilbur! Actually, my name is…"

"Are you finished?" Pip stood on Joseph's shoulder with his fingers plugged in his ears afraid that the young boy would go into his long speech about his many names. "Please tell me you're finished!"

"You must excuse my furry friend, Caroline. Pip's a little frazzled because he's lost his tail, he's hungry, and he doesn't want to be tonight's dinner. We're on our way to Blackberry Bog, but before we go, I must warn you about Wilbur." Joseph sat down next to Caroline. "Be careful you don't run into him. He's furious on account of Pip was hungry, he was tired of rubbing his gurgling tummy, and he drank half a jug of goat's milk that belonged to Wilbur. If you see a crooked man tall as a giant's rake, with a long triangular face, jug-like ears, prominent nose and a patch over his left eye, run, run as fast as you can! He eats little boys for breakfast, little girls for lunch, and anyone he can find for dinner."

"Shh. I think she fell asleep" Pip whispered, snuggled in Joseph's front pyjama pocket. He pointed in the direction of the setting sun. "Head there, partner. I think I see the stone bridge Tommy the Tortoise was talking about just behind that tall tamarack tree."

Joseph and Pip looked down at the snoring caterpillar with the green trunks and the pink ribbon in her hair. "Goodbye, Caroline. It was a pleasure meeting you. Good luck and remember to stay away from Wilbur," Joseph whispered.

"Quick, to the bridge," said Pip. "We're off to meet an alligator!

Furless Felix

A-*hink-a-honk-a-hink-a-honk* startled the pair as they made their way towards the stone bridge. They looked up through the dense canopy and spotted a green goose wearing a white bowtie diving down through the clouds.

"Look out, Sprout!" Pip shouted. "It's headed right for us!"

The goose pulled up and hovered above Joseph and Pip. "Cross now, cross now, Ollie's gone fishing." It fluttered and honked. "Cross now, cross now, Ollie's gone fishing."

"What on earth is going on?" Joseph shook his head and watched the goose fly away and disappear into the trees. "All I did was eat some garbanzo beans and now I'm listening to a green goose wearing a white bowtie, I'm cautioned by an orange caterpillar wearing bathing trunks and sunglasses, I'm talking to a 600-year-old tortoise wearing a scuba mask and snorkel, I'm humming along with a whistling ladybug holding a polka-dotted umbrella, I'm making deals with a chubby dormouse, I'm being scolded by a black-and-white checkered lizard, I'm being questioned by three swallows wearing top hats and white gloves, I'm searching for a Billy Goat with a long white beard and dark-rimmed glasses, I'm discussing life with an enormous tomcat wearing a striped tie and four different coloured sneakers, I might be eaten by a crooked old man tall as a giant's rake, and now I'm searching for an alligator named Allie. Emma would love to see this!"

Joseph and Pip crossed the stone bridge and noticed a yellow hummingbird swinging happily in a cradle made from a polished walnut shell. The cradle was tied to the branch of a majestic red maple tree. The hummingbird held a leash made from the silky thread of a black widow spider. At the end of the leash a glowing plump firefly buzzed back and forth.

"Hello down there," said the hummingbird.

"Hello up there," Joseph replied. "I wish bug-eyed Noah could see me now! He'd be so jealous," he muttered.

"Did you speak to Gregory the Goose, my friends?"

"Yes, well, not actually speak, but we listened."

"Good. My name is Henry and this is Francis. You need to hurry and cross to the other side of the bridge. You haven't got much time. It's almost that time when the sun kisses the horizon and Ollie the grumpy, frumpy, crabby, flabby, wheezing, sneezing ogre returns from his daily fishing trip. Ollie gets mighty angry when someone crosses his bridge."

Henry took a deep breath.

"The last to cross the ogre's bridge was Felix the Cat. Ollie caught Felix, tied him to a pole, and threw him into Lazy River. Felix was found three months later.

He floated downstream for a month before plummeting down Zorak Falls and then was pecked at for two months by a group of nasty soprano seagulls and a group of migrating laughing lobsters, until poor Felix had no fur left. Furless Felix is now the laughingstock of the neighbourhood. He's constantly looking up in the sky for soprano seagulls and then down at his feet for laughing lobsters."

Pip looked up at the sky and then down at this feet. "I hate singing seagulls, and I really hate laughing lobsters!" He nosedived into Joseph's pyjama pocket, his quivering, tail-less behind sticking out. "Please hurry, Sprout! It's getting dark and we've got to get to Blackberry Bog!"

Henry the Hummingbird's wings started beating a mile a minute. "Quick, the sun is almost kissing the horizon! Blackberry Bog is across that river. Once across, travel down the first hill, turn left at the second windmill and then turn right at the stable where Betsy the Cow used to live. Follow the dirt road up, down, up and then down again. There, you'll see a well. Beside the well is a sign with a yellow arrow pointing down. Look down and you'll see a white line painted across the path. Step over that line and you'll be in Blackberry Bog."

Frances the Firefly buzzed around. "Hurry, Ollie the grumpy, frumpy, crabby, flabby, wheezing, sneezing ogre will soon be here," Frances warned. "And don't forget to call out to Allie the Alligator. She'll get you safely across the river. Once across, you'll have all the time you need because time stands still on that side. There the sun never ever sets, the stars never ever shine, the clouds never ever move, and the moon always hangs in the western sky."

"I wish Ma and Pa and Grandpa and Seth and Jacob and Jeremiah and Miss Cameron and especially Emma were here to see this amazing place called Zorak," Joseph said. "I really wish that bug-eyed Noah could see me now. He'd be so jealous."

"One last thing before you go," Henry said.

"Oh, please don't ask how the boy got here, please!" Pip pleaded, slapping his forehead.

"I was going to ask if you know how to call Allie the Alligator?"

"I'll holler her name. I'll cry her name. I'll scream her name. I'll shout her name. I'll bellow her name. I'll screech her name. I'll bark her name. I'll shriek her name. I'll even howl her name," Pip squeaked. He looked across the river and sighed. "I just want to get across as fast as I can! I really, really need to get back my tail, and then I really, really want to help Sprout find his way back home!"

"What's all this about a tail?" asked Henry.

"There's a crooked old man who lives in the steeple. He's furious on account that my friend Pip was hungry, he was tired of rubbing his gurgling tummy, and he drank half a jug of goat's milk that belonged to Wilbur," Joseph explained. "Now he has Pip's tail. If you see a crooked old man tall as a giant's rake, with a long triangular face, jug-like ears, prominent nose and a patch over his left eye, run, run as fast as you can! He eats little boys for breakfast, little girls for lunch, and anyone he can find for dinner."

"What a fright it would be to meet him!" exclaimed Henry the Hummingbird grimacing and ruffling his feathers.

"If by sundown Wilbur's jug is not full of fresh milk, then I can forget about getting back my pencil-thin pink tail and my friend will never get back to Grandpa's farm!" Pip's voice trembled, his cheeks turned beet red, and his nose began to twitch. "At sundown we'll all be invited to dine with Wilbur and on the menu is us—roasted dormouse and boy stew. Please Henry, tell us how to call Allie the Alligator," pleaded Pip turning and staring at where his long, pink, beautiful tail used to be.

"Listen carefully! I only have time to say this once, so remember these instructions. At the edge of the river you'll see an old gnarled walnut tree—it's the only walnut tree in all of Zorak. In a hole in the trunk, you'll find a flute. The flute has only three stops. Blow on the flute and play one-three-three-one, two-one-two, one-three-three-one and two-one-two. Repeat this three times." Henry stopped, took a deep breath, and then continued. "Place the flute back in the hole and count to six. Then clap your hands twice and call out 'Allie the Alligator come out, come out, wherever you are!' Count backwards from six to one and Allie will be by the edge of the river. Step onto Allie's back and she'll take you across. Once across, you'll know what to do."

"We will?" Joseph said.

"We will, we will!" Pip cried out taking Joseph by the hand and pulling him towards the river. "Let's hurry, Sprout! We still have to cross the bridge, travel down the first hill, turn left at the second windmill, turn right at the stable where Betsy the Cow used to live, follow the dirt road up, down, up and then down again." Pip wiped the sweat off his brow, stared at Joseph and sighed. "Then, if and when we find the well, we have to look for the sign with a yellow arrow pointing down, look down and cross the white painted line and step over into Blackberry Bog."

Joseph and Pip crossed the stone bridge and turned to wave goodbye to Henry the Hummingbird and Francis the Firefly. They saw only an empty cradle and then heard loud sneezing and wheezing echoing throughout the valley.

"Ollie the grumpy, frumpy, crabby, flabby, wheezing, sneezing ogre must have returned," Joseph whispered.

"I got a good look at Ollie as you were stepping off the bridge." Pip stood up on shaky legs with widened eyes. "He's ugly, he's ghastly, he's utterly horrific, Sprout! He's like a mouldy glop of creepy crawly gelatine. He has two gigantic bulging white eyes with thick blue veins crisscrossing his pupils. He's bald, full of oozing moles, and has the biggest, reddest, flabbiest, floppiest drooling lips you've ever seen. He has bony knees, short sinewy legs, and feet as large as two frying pans. Golly he's ugly

Sprout. Ollie the Ogre is uglier than a mud fence, he is."

"Look!" Joseph shouted and pointed. "There's the gnarled walnut tree and there's the river's edge. We're here!"

"We're a team, Sprout. Boy oh boy, what a team we make!"

Pip inserted his orange hand into the hole in the tree, pulled out the flute and handed it to Joseph. "You play the flute and I'll call out the notes. I remember them. Yes, I do. One-three-three-one, two-one-two, one-three-three-one, two-one-two."

A Babbling Brook

Joseph played the notes on the flute and looked for any movement in Lazy River.

"One more time," Pip said. "Nice and loud. One-three-three-one, two-one-two, one-three-three-one, two-one-two."

Joseph finished playing the notes and placed the flute back into the tree hole. Pip shouted "one, two, three, four, five, six" and clapped his hands twice. "Allie the Alligator come out, come out, wherever you are!"

Joseph shouted out, "Six, five, four, three, two, one."

"Hey, look, there she is." Pip jumped up and down on Joseph's shoulder and pointed. "Hello, Allie!"

Joseph carefully boarded the alligator's bumpy green back, thinking "Emma would love to see this!" He and Pip floated safely across the river to where the sun never ever sets, the stars never ever shine, the clouds never ever move, and the moon always hangs in the western sky. Joseph gingerly stepped off Allie's back and onto the rocky shore. He and Pip waved goodbye as Allie glided across Lazy River, back towards the gnarled walnut tree. Allie turned, snapped her powerful jaws twice, and then disappeared under the calm, flowing waters of the river.

"See you later, alligator!" Joseph and Pip said in unison.

They journeyed down the first hill and turned left at the second windmill, and then turned right at the stable where Betsy the Cow used to live. "Hey Pip, is this the same Betsy that jumped over the moon?"

"That's right, partner. She jumped the night China the Dish ran away with Scoop the Spoon. Poor Betsy was never ever seen again."

They followed the dirt road up and down, then up and down again. "Hey, there's the well and there's the sign with the yellow arrow pointing down." Pip's eyes widened. "Look! There's the white line painted across the path."

"All we have to do is step over that line," Joseph said, "and we're in Blackberry Bog!" Let's stop here by this babbling brook, Sprout." They sat down beside a large maple tree. "I'm awfully tired and it still looks a good distance away. You look like you could use some rest, too."

"In Blackberry Bog, tomorrow or yesterday doesn't exist. Today is tomorrow and yesterday is today. Tomorrow or yesterday doesn't exist. Today is tomorrow and yesterday is today."

Joseph and Pip looked at each other. "Who said that?" they said at the same time. Pip scurried onto Joseph's shoulder, hopped on his head, and looked about, trying to identify the person behind the strange voice.

"In Blackberry Bog, tomorrow or yesterday doesn't exist. Today is tomorrow and yesterday is today. Tomorrow or yesterday doesn't exist. Today is tomorrow and yesterday is today."

"It's coming from that babbling brook Sprout. Listen."

"In Blackberry Bog, tomorrow or yesterday doesn't exist. Today is tomorrow and yesterday is today. Tomorrow or yesterday doesn't exist. Today is tomorrow and yesterday is today."

"I think the babbling brook is telling us that time stands still on this side of the river, just like Henry the Hummingbird told us, remember?" Joseph said. "Here the sun never ever sets, the stars never ever shine, the clouds never ever move, and the moon always hangs in the western sky."

Joseph brought his knees up to his chest, clutched his legs, and closed his tired eyes. He listened to the repetitive chant of the babbling brook. His heavy eyelids closed and his head flopped. Pip curled up in Joseph's pyjama pocket and fell asleep with him.

Look Who's Coming Down River

Joseph and Pip woke up, startled and hungry, to an incessant warning coming from Lazy River.

"If the log rolls over, we'll all be dead! If the log rolls over, we'll all be dead!"

"I think we better hide!" Pip nosedived back into Joseph's pyjama pocket to take cover. "It doesn't sound good!" his voice quivered.

"If the log rolls over, we'll all be dead! If the log rolls over, we'll all be dead!"

The incessant, threatening prattle was accompanied by the constant chant of the nearby babbling brook. "In Blackberry Bog, tomorrow or yesterday doesn't exist. Today is tomorrow and yesterday is today. Tomorrow or yesterday doesn't exist. Today is tomorrow and yesterday is today."

"Hurry, Sprout, let's hide!" Pip shouted.

"Don't you worry your little tail off, my fury, chubby Cuz."

Pip looked to his left, and then to his right. "Who's calling me cousin?"

"It's just those banana-eating-card-playing-no-good-for-nothing mischievous monkeys crossing the Lazy River," said a voice.

Joseph stared up at the walnut tree. "Who's there?"

"It's me, Patches." A black possum with two patches of white fur around bulging red eyes swung on a branch from his thick black-and-white striped tail. "There's absolutely nothing to worry about, little Cuz and Blondie Blue Eyes."

Joseph looked back at Pip. "I guess there's nothing to worry about. That's what your cousin is telling us."

"What cousin? I don't have any cousin living in Zorak. Don't be foolish Sprout. And if I did," Pip said, pointing up at the possum, "he wouldn't be swinging upside-down from his tail and he certainly wouldn't look like that!"

"Hey Cuz. No need to get upset! I'm simply telling you that you're hearing the rant of those banana-eating-card-playing-cigar-smoking-no-good-for-nothing mischievous monkeys who live on the other side of Lazy River, where the sun never ever sets, the stars never ever shine, the clouds never ever move and the moon always hangs in the western sky."

Patches swung upright and sat on the branch.

"Every day at about this time, they hop on a log and cross the river to continue their mischievous ways. They always chant the same thing. 'If the log rolls over, we'll all be dead! If the log rolls over, we'll all be dead!" Boy, what a bunch of loudmouths. They always manage—all twelve of them—to safely cross. Allie the Alligator no longer pays any attention to them. She's tired of their antics, and so is everyone else. Got it, Cuz? Got it, Blondie Blue Eyes?"

Joseph stared up at the possum when he heard he was being called Blondie Blue Eyes. "I wish bug-eyed Noah could see me now! He'd be so jealous."

"My name isn't Blondie Blue Eyes. Actually, my name is..."

Pip stuck his fingers in his ears.

"But what on earth are you doing on this side of Lazy River? And where is your tail, Blondie Blue Eyes?" responded Patches.

Pip's ears remained plugged, so Joseph replied on his behalf.

"There's a crooked old man who lives in the steeple on the other side of the river. He's furious on account that my friend Pip was hungry, he was tired of rubbing his gurgling tummy, and he drank half a jug of goat's milk that belonged to Wilbur. Now he has Pip's tail. If you ever see a crooked old man tall as a giant's rake, with a long triangular face, jug-like ears, prominent nose and a patch over his left eye, run, run as fast as you can! He eats little boys for breakfast, little girls for lunch, and anyone he can find for dinner. If by sundown the jug is not full of fresh milk, then Pip can forget about getting back his pencil-thin pink tail! At sundown, we'll be invited to dine with Wilbur and on the menu is us—roasted dormouse and boy stew."

"And what," asked Patches, "are you doing in Zorak, Blondie Blue Eyes... I mean, Joseph? I've been hearing stories about you tumbling down a mountain and crashing into a fence. Everyone's talking about it. Is it t true?"

Before anyone could say anything about falling and crashing and mountains and fences and frightening journeys, Pip pointed to the white line on the path and shouted, "There it is! Quick, step over the white line and we'll finally be in Blackberry Bog. Hurray! We've made it!"

Looking like a Jack-o-lantern

Joseph's feet sunk into the wet, spongy, mossy ground as he and Pip stepped deeper into Blackberry Bog and the dense canopy of the valley slowly disappeared. Old gnarled trees made way to small shrubs filled with black, red, and white berries. The open space revealed a full yellow moon hanging in the eastern sky, frozen white clouds, and a large orange sun glowing just over the horizon in the western sky.

"Hello is anybody here?" shouted Pip.

"Hello? Buffy can you hear us?" shrieked Joseph, his feet squelching, squashing, and squishing in the marshy bog. Shivers crawled up his spine and goose bumps covered his arms. He tucked his hands deep into his pyjama pant pockets, intently studied the muddy ground, and recognized several plants.

"Grandpa picks similar herbs in the valley and stores them in glass jars atop the pantry," he told Pip. "Ma picks those to make fragrant baskets on special occasions. They smell like vanilla. I think Ma calls it sweet grass. And Grandpa picks those sweet-smelling, cheery-blue flowers when our tummies are sore."

"My ma fed me dry water iris too, when I ate too much and I thought I was going to explode," Pip said, rubbing his tummy.

"I certainly believe that." Joseph chuckled and poked Pip's stomach. "You must have eaten a lot of blue water iris, Pip—look at your drooping tummy!"

Dark green creeping groundcover with shiny double yellow flowers cascaded over fallen logs and boulders.

"My, what beautiful buttercups, Sprout!"

"I hate buttercups, Pip. Ma rubs them all over our skin. She says they will help our bones grow strong and prevent warts. My friend Noah once told me to hold a buttercup under my chin. Then he laughed at me saying that my chin was yellow and that meant I was in love." Joseph's cheeks turned beet red when he thought of Emma, with the long chestnut hair and the fancy dark blue pinafore, staring at him in the classroom.

"Excuse me, where are you going? I'm speaking to you, Pyjama Boy!"

"Buffy!" shouted Joseph. "Are we glad, to see you!"

"Oh, so now you're speaking to goats, are you?

"Please don't be upset with me, Buffy. I do believe I've talked to a dormouse and goat and a tomcat and a lizard and swallows and a tortoise and a ladybug and a hummingbird and a possum and a caterpillar. I...we need your help."

"Well, well, well, what have we here? I see the foolish little boy with the missing front teeth and his chubby little mouse made it out of Wilbur's steeple all in one piece." Larry the Lizard crawled beside Buffy, rapidly flicking his tongue.

"Why, hello Larry. Would you please help Pip and me? Please, pretty please?"

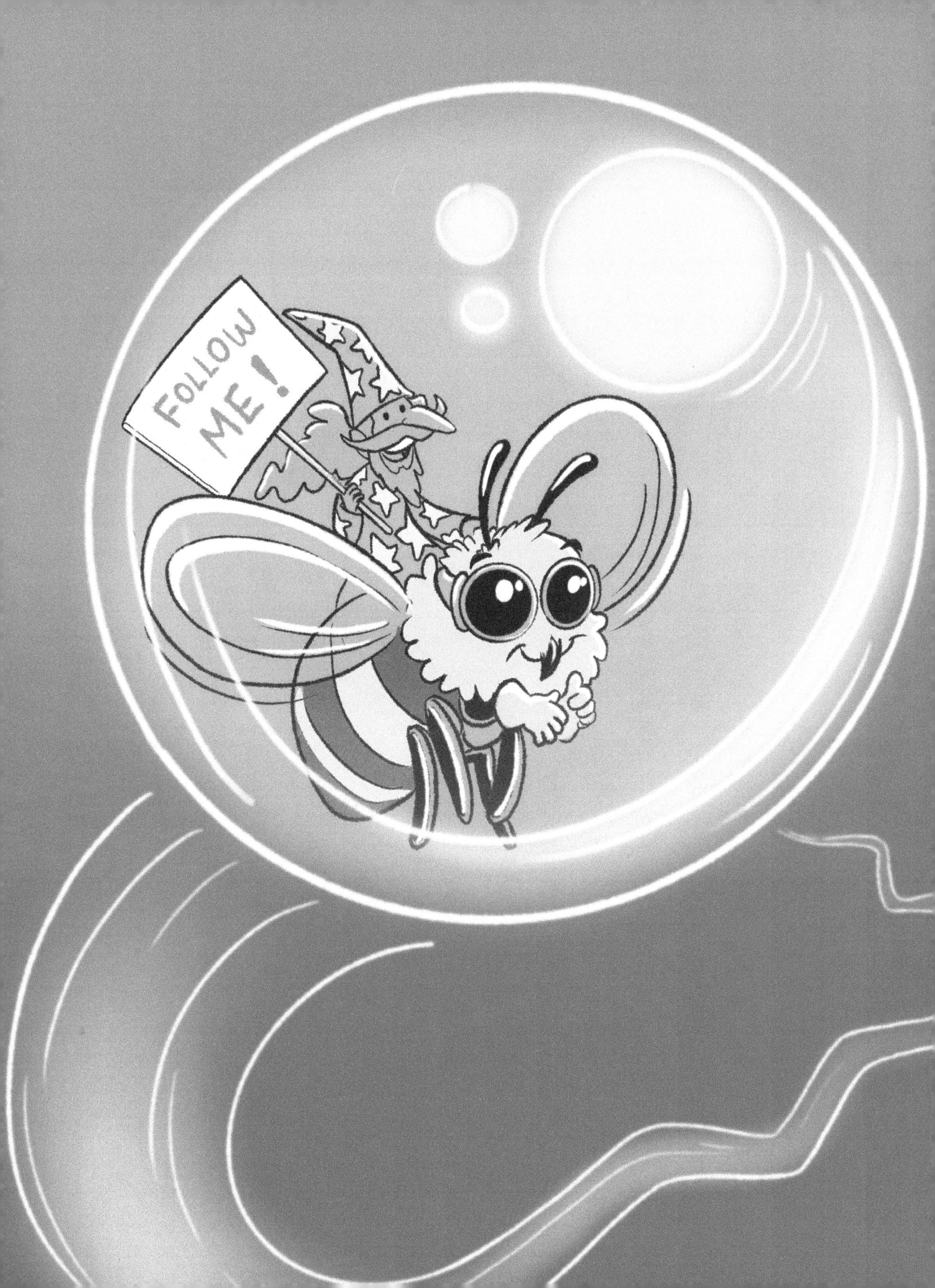
FOLLOW
ME!

"You're still talking like a little ten-year-old, I see. Are you going to say, 'Pretty please with sugar on top?' "

"Why are you so mean, Larry?"

"Yeah why are you so mean," Pip chimed in.

Buffy butted his head against a fallen log and then sat down on a flat rock.

"Please everyone, stop shouting." He crossed his legs, put on his dark-rimmed glasses, and stroked his long white beard. "What kind of help do you want from me?"

"We have travelled far and wide to come to Blackberry Bog to ask for your help Buffy," responded Joseph. "We need goat's milk to take to Wilbur, and then Wilbur will give Pip his tail back, and Pip can help me find my way home."

Larry the Lizard stood on his hind two legs. "I told you they're dumber than a bag of nails Buffy." He shook his head. "Let's get out of here. We want nothing to do with Wilbur or this scrawny kid or this chubby tail-less mouse."

"Wait, not so fast! Let me think about this for a moment." Buffy the Billy Goat pursed his lips and rubbed his chin. "Listen Pyjama Boy, why should I help you? What have you ever done for me?"

"Answer him!" Larry shouted. "Don't just stand there staring with your mouth open. You look like a jack-o-lantern."

Pip sunk into Joseph's pyjama pocket and curled up into a ball. Joseph squelched and squashed and squished over to Buffy. He sat down cross-legged beside him. "What *is* it that I can do for you, Buffy?"

"I'd like fresh grass to eat." Buffy stood up. "Get me some fresh grass, I'll get you some fresh goat's milk—deal?"

"We're wasting our time on these two," Larry said. "They're totally loose screws. I think they're so dumb they'd take a duck to a chicken fight. Let's move on."

Joseph stared into Buffy's eyes. "It's a deal! I'll definitely find you some fresh grass to eat."

Pip stood up in Joseph's pyjama pocket, smacked his forehead, and mouthed, "Where are we going to find fresh grass in a bog?"

Joseph stood up and trudged away disappointed, feeling lower than a bow-legged caterpillar. His feet squelched and squashed and squished along the soggy bog.

"We'll be back with some fresh grass," he vowed over his shoulder. "We don't know when, but we'll be back."

"Joseph, look up!" Pip leaped onto Joseph's shoulder and jumped up and down.

"I thought you were asleep in my pyjama pocket, Pip? What are you doing hopping like a jackrabbit?"

"Look up, Sprout!"

A brilliant soap bubble the size of a cantaloupe floated down in a zigzag pattern. A skinny wizard with blazing red hair, wearing spurs on his boots, rode a striped bumblebee wearing goggles and leather gloves. The wizard held a sign in his left hand that said, "Follow me!"

"Follow him... I mean them, Sprout," Pip said excitedly. "Follow that bronco-busting, red-haired wizard!"

"Okay, Pip!" Staring in amazement Joseph muttered, "Emma would love to see this!"

They followed the brilliant soap bubble with the small wizard riding the striped bumblebee along winding trails, under stone bridges, across babbling brooks, through thorny brambles, among drooping cattails, between large bluffs and through a dry meadow of yellow grass. A small cottage with gingerbread trim, wooden shutters, and a wrap-a-round veranda stood in middle of the meadow.

"The wizard is writing something on his sign." Pip pointed to the brilliant soap bubble hovering over the front stoop. Joseph stared at the smiling bumblebee wearing goggles and leather gloves, and then at the red-haired wizard pointing to his sign. The sign read "Knock on door... goodbye, my friends."

Let's Make a Deal

Joseph tiptoed up to the door of the cottage. He knocked and sat down silently on the front stoop, waiting patiently with Pip in his pyjama pocket. They heard the thumping of hooves from inside the cottage, and then the banging of doors and the crashing of plates. Joseph stood up and faced the front door as it screeched open. A donkey wearing green galoshes and a yellow raincoat, chewing on a blade of grass, stepped out onto the porch and opened a red umbrella.

"Is it raining yet?" she said in a long, drawn-out voice.

"Excuse us, madam. My name is Joseph and this here is my friend Pip. May we have some fresh grass from your meadow?"

"Well, is it raining or isn't it?"

"No, madam, it is not," Pip replied.

"Well then, I'm afraid that I cannot give you any grass, chubby." The donkey spoke to Pip but stared up and down at Joseph.

"If it was raining, then could you give us some grass?" Joseph asked. Before listening to the answer he muttered, "I wish bug-eyed Noah could see me now! He'd be so jealous."

"Who are you two and why are you standing on my porch?"

"Good day, madam." Pip jumped up on Joseph's head and bowed. "This here is Sprout and my name is Pip—not Chubby. We need goat's milk to give to the crooked old man who lives in the steeple in Zorak. Old Man Wilbur is furious on account that I was hungry, I was tired of rubbing my gurgling tummy, and I drank some goat's milk that belonged to him. He tried to grab me, I escaped his grip, but he still had my tail in his hand. He said if we replace the goat's milk by sundown, he would give me back my pencil-thin tail. If not, we'll be invited to dine with Wilbur and on the menu is us—roasted dormouse and boy stew."

"If we don't replace the milk, Pip won't get back his tail and I won't make it back home to Grandpa's farm," Joseph added.

"And what does all this have to do with me?" The donkey stomped and brayed on her front stoop.

"Well, it's long story that involves an alligator named Allie, a goat named Buffy, his mean friend Larry the Lizard, and a tiny red-haired wizard wearing spurs on his boots riding a striped bumblebee wearing goggles and leather gloves floating in a brilliant soap bubble..." Pip's voice trailed off.

"I don't know anybody named Allie or Buffy or Larry, but yes, I know Scribbles the Wizard," the donkey replied. "Scribbles has lived in Blackberry Bog with his pet bumblebee Honey for 7,000 years... but I still don't understand."

"Perhaps I can explain," Joseph interjected.

"And who exactly are *you* Barefooted Boy?" The donkey stomped and snorted as Pip leaped onto Joseph's shoulder and stuffed his fingers in his ears.

"My name isn't Barefooted Boy. Actually my name is..."

"My name is Doris. How did you end up on my porch, Barefooted Boy? Is it true what they're saying? Is it true that you came rolling down a mountain and crashed into Zorak?"

"Yes...yes it's truer than true. It was a crazy journey. Just crazy... and scary."

"You sure do talk a lot," Doris brayed, bobbing her head up and down. "So, you're looking for some fresh grass. Why?"

"We went looking for Buffy the Billy Goat to get goat's milk, and when we finally met up with him, he refused. Buffy said, 'Get me some fresh grass; I'll get you some fresh milk.' So I made the deal and here I am, asking you for fresh grass."

"My, that must have been some fall into Zorak my little friend," Doris brayed. "Everyone knows fresh water makes for a green meadow, and a green meadow makes for fresh grass. So let's make a deal, too, shall we? Get me some water from Blackberry Bog's old fresh-water fountain for my meadow—and the water must come from the fountain, I can taste the difference—and I'll give you fresh grass for Buffy. The Billy Goat will give you fresh milk, and then Wilbur the crooked old man will give you back Pip's tail, and your chubby little friend will help you find your way back home—deal?"

Joseph stepped down the front stoop disappointed, feeling lower than a bow-legged caterpillar.

"We'll be back with some fresh water from Blackberry Bog's old fresh-water fountain," he vowed over his shoulder. "We don't know when, but we'll be back."

Pip stood up in Joseph's pocket, smacked his forehead, and mouthed, "Where are we going to find a fresh-water fountain in a bog?"

"I'll be waiting." Doris the Donkey closed her umbrella. "Goodbye and good luck."

Wouldn't Hurt a Fly

Joseph continued along the dry yellow meadow and climbed a steep hill that overlooked a magnificent gorge ablaze with colour. Pip peeked out of Joseph's pocket, covered a large floppy pink ear with a hand, and shrieked, "Speak up, Joseph, I can't hear you!"

"I didn't say a thing." Joseph came to a halt. "Where do we go from here? Have any ideas?"

As Pip prepared to answer, a spiny black warthog with a pair of tusks protruding from its mouth and curving upwards ran out of the tall grass on hind legs.

"Come on, come on! Put up your hands!" it whooped. "Put 'em up! I'm ready for a fight!"

The warthog, wearing a red bandana around its head, running shoes on its back hooves, and a pair of boxing gloves on its front hooves, shuffled its feet on the dusty ground and sparred with the vacant air.

"Left jab. Left jab followed by a right uppercut! Left jab. Left jab followed by a right uppercut!"

Pip stood tall in Joseph's pocket, shuffled his feet, and sparred back. "You get any closer I'll punch you so hard you'll fall into next week, you smelly hog! Come on, put 'em up! Put 'em up!"

Frightened at the sight of the sparring dormouse, the warthog dropped its gloved hands and cowered behind a mulberry bush. "Hey, I was only joking—honest I was." It poked its head out and shielded its eyes with its left arm. "Could you please tell your ferocious, chubby little friend to settle down? I was only joking—honest I was."

"This tough little fella is Pip, and I'm Joseph." He walked over to the mulberry bush and offered his hand to the warthog. "There's nothing to worry about, Mr. Warthog. Pip wouldn't hurt you. I promise." Joseph stared in awe and muttered, "Emma would love to see this!"

"Well, as long as you promise." The warthog cautiously tiptoed out from behind the bush and vigilantly accepted Joseph's hand. "My name is Wally. As you can see, I'm a warthog—although I've always wanted to be a boxer. Hello, Joseph. Hello, Pip."

"Can you tell us where we can find the old fresh-water fountain?" Pip asked in a curt tone. "We're in a hurry!"

"Did you say old fresh-water fountain? Because that's what I think I heard you say."

"Which way is it, you smelly hog?" Pip squeaked.

"Please Pip, don't be angry with me. I was only joking with my sparring and my fancy footwork—honest I was. I couldn't... I wouldn't... hurt anyone, not even a fly—honest I wouldn't." Wally the Warthog pointed down the hill to the magnificent gorge that was all ablaze with colour. "Why on earth would you risk your lives?"

"Risk our lives? Who said anything about risking our lives?" Joseph said.

"Yeah, who said anything about risking our lives, Stinky?" Pip stood on Joseph's shoulder, chewed on a blade of grass, and rubbed his drooping tummy.

"We need fresh water to bring to Doris the Donkey." Joseph knelt on the ground, rubbed Wally's snout, and stood back up. "Then we'll be on our way."

Pip leaned against Joseph's cheek and whispered, "Jeepers Sprout, this Wally smells so bad he could make an onion cry. Phew!" He pinched his nose and held his breath.

"Why do you need water from the old fresh-water fountain, when there are so many brooks and streams?" Wally asked.

"It's a long story Smelly," Pip said tersely. "But if you really, really want to know, we need goat's milk to give to the crooked old man who lives in the steeple in Zorak. Old Man Wilbur is furious on account that I was hungry, I was tired of rubbing my gurgling tummy, and I drank some goat's milk that belonged to him. He grabbed me. I managed to escape his grip but he still had my tail in his hand. He said if we replace the goat's milk by sundown, he would give me back my pencil-thin tail. We went looking for Buffy the Billy Goat to ask for goat's milk, and when we finally met up with him, he refused. Buffy said, 'Get me some fresh grass and I'll get you some fresh milk.' Sprout and I made a deal with Buffy that we would find him some fresh grass. We searched for Doris the Donkey and she said that everyone knows fresh water makes for a green meadow, and a green meadow makes fresh grass. So, we made a deal with Doris that we would get her water from Blackberry Bog's old fresh-water fountain for her meadow. She said if we did, she would give us fresh grass for Buffy, and we could bring it to the Billy Goat, and he'd give us goat's milk. Old Man Wilbur said if we replaced the goat's milk by sundown, he would give me back my pencil-thin tail. If not, we'd be invited to dine with Wilbur and on the menu is us—roasted dormouse and boy stew!"

Pip leaned against Joseph's cheek, totally exhausted. "Did you get all that Stinky?"

"If we don't replace the milk, Pip won't get back his tail and I won't make it back home to Grandpa's farm," Joseph added. "So here we are asking a smelly warthog for directions to get to the old fresh-water fountain."

"I'll take you to the old fresh-water fountain if you promise to protect me from the grotesque troll who lives under the fountain," Willie the Warthog responded. "Tar the Troll used to live in the tombs under a very old cathedral. Legend has it that the din of the church bells drove Tar to this side of the river. He's lived alone under the old fresh-water fountain for 44,444 years."

"Let's get cracking!" Pip barked. "There's no time to waste. We have a very old troll named Tar to visit!"

"Don't worry Wally, we'll protect you," Joseph said over his shoulder as the sparring warthog followed. "I promise."

"I don't think Tar the Troll would want to get closer than a country mile to that stinky, smelly warthog," Pip whispered to Joseph and faked a smile at Wally. "Ugh! That hog stinks so bad he could knock a buzzard off a gut wagon."

"Hey Pip, you know what they say, don't you? A fake smile hides a million tears."

"Right you are, partner. That pungent hog smell brings nothing but tears to my eyes. Now let's hurry!"

Over bush and over dale, through bush and through briar, across meadow and across brook, along riverbed and along wood fence, up knoll and uphill, between bluff and between cliff, down gorge and down dusty trail, Joseph and Pip and Wally journeyed without stopping, without talking. Huffing and puffing and gasping and panting they finally reached the old fresh-water fountain.

Wally suddenly stopped dead in his tracks, shuffled his feet, and started to spar in the air.

"Left jab. Left jab followed by a right uppercut! Left jab. Left jab followed by a right uppercut!"

A tremendous roar sent them cowering behind a fallen log. "Protect me, Joseph. Protect me, Pip!" Wally shouted.

"Who dare approach my fountain?" The earth shook and quaked from the thunderous voice and the wall of the fresh-water fountain collapsed. "Go back where you came from! Go back or you'll be tied to a stake, your eyes will be poked out with a sharp pole, your fingernails will be ripped out, your fingers and toes will be broken one by one, and your ears will be pulled out of your head. And then, if you're still breathing, you'll be tickled until your heart jumps out of your mouth and your ribcage collapses—go back!"

"Yikes, that's Tar. I'm outta here!" Wally the Warthog ran on his hind legs punching the air with his gloved hands. "I couldn't… I wouldn't… hurt anyone, not even a fly. See you later, folks."

Pip stared up at Joseph and chuckled. "So much for our ferocious, smelly, stinky friend Wally the wannabe-boxer Warthog. It's up to us to get fresh water for Doris the Donkey."

"Listen, Pip!" Joseph pointed to a stone structure up ahead of them.

Tickled to Death

"Go back to where you came from! Go back or you'll be tied to a stake, your eyes will be poked out with a sharp pole, your fingernails will be ripped out, your fingers and toes will be broken one by one, and your ears will be pulled out of your head. And then, if you're still breathing, you'll be tickled until your heart jumps out of your mouth and your ribcage collapses—go back!"

"Oh please, Mr. Troll," Joseph shouted, "give us some water from the fresh-water fountain to give to Doris the Donkey for her meadow, and then she'll give us fresh grass for Buffy, and then he'll give us fresh milk for Wilbur, and then the crooked old man will give back Pip's tail, and then Pip can then help me find my way back to Grandpa's farm." Awaiting a response Joseph muttered, "I wish bug-eyed Noah could see me now! He'd be so jealous."

"How dare you interrupt my sleep Silly Boy!" bellowed Tar the Troll. "Nobody has interrupted my sleep for 44,444 years. Go back!"

"My name isn't Silly Boy. Actually my name is..."

Joseph took a deep breath. "I'm ten years old and I live with my family on Grandpa's Farm. I'm lost. I'm hungry. Can you help me? I don't know why I'm here or how I got here. I don't know what I'm doing speaking to a hummingbird and a lizard and a tortoise and sparrows and a goat and a donkey and a warthog and a now a troll. I just want to go home. May I please have some water, Mr. Troll?"

"Go away, Silly Boy! Why should I give you any water?" Tar the Troll snickered. "Go on, do tell. Have you ever helped me with anything? Well, have you, Silly Boy?"

"Tar, we can't see you, but we can certainly hear you." Pip jumped on top of Joseph's head. "You're as loud as a horn!"

Joseph climbed to his feet and continued speaking towards the toppled fountain. "What is it that we can do for you Tar? Tell us and we'll make you a deal for some of your water."

"If you can find a mason to fix my fountain, I might give you the water you ask for."

"So, if we find a mason to fix your toppled fountain, you promise to give us fresh water to take to Doris the Donkey? Then she will give us fresh grass to give to Buffy, and he will give us goat's milk for the crooked old man who lives in the steeple. Old Man Wilbur will give back Pip's tail and then Pip can help me find my way back to Grandpa's farm."

"Okay, okay, stop your talking! Please, stop," Tar bellowed. "Now get out of here and let me get back to sleep. Don't you dare interrupt me again—understood?"

Pip stood up in Joseph's pocket, smacked his forehead, and mouthed, "Where are we going to find a mason in a bog?"

Joseph trudged away from the fresh-water fountain disappointed, feeling lower than a bow-legged caterpillar.

"We'll be back with a mason Tar," Joseph vowed over his shoulder. "We don't know when, but we'll be back."

Joseph looked at Pip. "Where do we go from here? Have any ideas? Maybe we should just go back to Old Man Wilbur and beg for your tail back."

"Come on, partner, pull yourself up from your bootstraps and let's find us a mason," Pip declared.

Joseph looked down at his muddy bare feet.

"You're right, Pip! Going back to Wilbur without any goat's milk is definitely out of the question! Why, I'd rather jump barefooted off a six-foot stepladder into a five-gallon bucket full of porcupine quills than go back to that crooked, triangular-faced, jug-eared, patch-wearing, jaw harp-playing, seed-spitting, child-eating, nose-hair-plucking, whistling brute."

"Right you are, partner! Even though I feel like twenty pounds of lard stuffed in a ten-pound sack right now, I would rather drink his bathwater than beg Wilbur. I hate that crooked old man and that oversized tomcat who purrs like a tractor!"

"Why does Acorn stay with Wilbur? Is she that dumb?" Joseph said.

"I think Acorn is so dumb that if dumb were dirt, she'd cover about an acre."

Joseph slapped his thigh and laughed. "Come on, Pip, Acorn's not that dumb."

"No?" Pip buried his long, thick snout into Joseph's cheek. "Why, if you gave her two nickels for a dime, she'd think she was rich."

They both hooted with laughter.

"Come on, partner," Joseph said, "let's find us a mason."

That's What Friends Are For

The glowing orange sun stood still on the horizon, the hazy moon sat in the western sky, and the motionless clouds hung low over Blackberry Bog as Joseph and Pip wandered aimlessly amid bramble and bush, cliff and stream, meadow and dale.

"Hey Pip, do you have any idea where we're going?"

"Absolutely, partner." Pip rubbed his drooping tummy and settled down into Joseph's warm pyjama pocket. "We're on our way to find a mason, right?"

"Right you are," Joseph replied. "I don't know about you, but I'm pooped, tired, bushed—and hungry!"

Joseph peeked into his pyjama pocket and spotted Pip already curled up and sleeping like a baby. He sat down on the ground cross-legged, leaned against a fallen log, and closed his eyes.

"Wow! This is the longest, most confusing and strangest dream I've ever had." He yawned and then wrapped his arms around his shoulders. "I sure wish I were in my bed right now."

Pip's soft snores lulled Joseph to sleep.

Moments later, ear-splitting screeches and grinding noises awakened Joseph and Pip. Pip stuck his head out of the pyjama pocket and pointed. "Look, Sprout—there's a chuck wagon coming along that trail. Maybe someone can tell us where we can find a mason in this neck of the woods—*if* one even exists."

Joseph grimaced and plugged his ears at the noisy approaching chuck wagon.

"I can't believe it, Sprout. No one's steering the wagon!" Pip said in astonishment. "A wagon—with no driver?"

The wagon came to a halt within inches of their feet. A large oak barrel was attached to the front of the wagon and a yellow canvas hung underneath stacked with loose logs. A small wooden chuck box with a hinged lid, two drawers, and one shelf was latched to the back. Pip gathered up his courage and hopped up into the bed of the covered wagon.

He found a bloodhound fast asleep amid cooking supplies, cowboy hats and boots, and sleeping bags. Cans of lima beans, a sack of coffee beans, some sourdough biscuits, and a wheel of cheese lined the wagon's two shelves. A square piece of salted pork hung from a metal hook in the centre of the wagon. Pip eyed the stored food and drooled. He hopped off the wagon, scurried over to Joseph, and licked his lips.

"In that there chuck wagon is a feast fit for a king—I mean a feast fit for two kings—King Pip and King Sprout," Pip informed Joseph. "There's also a dog in that there wagon. I think you look a little tired and hungry. I'm also tired and hungry. I think *we* need some grub right about now, don't you think?"

Joseph and Pip quietly hopped up on the wagon, trying not to wake the bloodhound.

"I'm not *only* the trail boss," the bloodhound barked, still half-asleep, his heavy voice stopping Joseph and Pip dead in their tracks. "I'm the trail boss *and* the cook on this here chuck wagon. I'm the barber, the dentist, and the banker. I'm Red the Hound."

The dog grunted, his long and narrow head nestled comfortably between two sacks of flour, and his long black and tan muzzle pointed upwards.

"Hello, Mr. Red," Joseph said in almost a whisper. Then waiting for a response he muttered, "Emma would love to see this!"

Annoyed at the dog and famished, Pip shouted, "Mr. Cook, Mr. Banker, Mr. Baker, Mr. Dentist, Mr. Red—how about you getting up and fixing us something to eat?"

"Who's there?" Red the Hound slumbered to his feet. Wrinkled skin hung loosely around his head and loose folds around his neck.

"Are you awake, Mr. Red? We're so sorry to bother you, but..."

"Don't waste your time speaking to this hound," Pip piped in. "Why he's so lazy, you'd have to look twice to see him move."

"Who are you and what are you doing in my wagon?" Red the Hound struggled to open his drooping eyelids. His ears were so long they brushed against the floor of the chuck wagon.

"We haven't eaten in a dog's age." Pip rubbed his belly. "How about sparing us some of them vittles? It looks like there's plenty to go around."

"Absolutely, definitely, surely indeed," Red the Hound replied in a gentle voice. "Help yourself to whatever you like—after all, that's what friends are for, right?"

"Absolutely, Mr. Red, sir." Pip dashed over to the shelf and began nibbling on the wheel of cheese. "That's what friends are for—exactly!"

Red the Hound finally managed to fully open his bloodshot eyes, lift his heavy head, and turn to Joseph. "So, Squirt, what's your name?"

"My name isn't Squirt. Actually, my name is ..."

He paused for a moment to look around the chuck wagon. "I'm ten years old and I live with my family on Grandpa's farm. I'm lost. I'm hungry. Can you help me? I don't know why I'm here or how I got here. I don't know what I'm doing speaking to a hummingbird and sparrows and a lizard and a tortoise and a goat and a wizard and a donkey and a warthog and a troll and now a bloodhound. I just want to go home."

"Well, how did you get here then, Squirt? And, don't tell me that ridiculous story I've been hearing about you falling down a mountain is true."

Pip looked up from his wheel of cheese, considered saying something to the dog or plugging his ears with his fingers, but then decided to go back to nibbling.

"Is certainly is true. It's truer than true," said Joseph.

"What can I do for you?" Red sniffed Joseph's pant leg. "What kind of help do you need from me?"

"There's a crooked old man who lives in the steeple on the other side of the Lazy River. He's furious on account that my friend Pip here was hungry, he was tired of rubbing his gurgling tummy, and he drank half a jug of goat's milk that belonged to Wilbur. He grabbed Pip. Pip managed to escape his grip but he still had Pip's tail in his hand. He said if we replaced the goat's milk by sundown, he would give Pip back his pencil-thin tail. We went looking for Buffy the Billy Goat to ask for goat's milk, and when we finally met up with him, he refused. Buffy said, 'Get me some fresh grass and I'll get you some fresh milk.' We made a deal with Buffy that we would find him fresh grass. We found Doris the Donkey thanks to a tiny wizard and a striped bumblebee and she said to us that everyone knows fresh water makes for a green meadow, and a green meadow makes for fresh grass. We made a deal with Doris that we would get water from Blackberry Bog's old fresh-water fountain for her meadow. She said if we did, she would give us fresh grass for Buffy, we'd bring it to the Billy Goat, and he'd give us the goat's milk. When we found the fresh-water fountain, we disturbed Tar the Troll who lives under it. He thundered and the wall collapsed. We made a deal with Tar that if we found a mason and fixed the wall, we could have water from the fountain, but he warned us not to disturb him ever again. Wilbur said if we replaced the goat's milk by sundown, he would give Pip back his pencil-thin tail and Pip would help me find my way home. If the jug is not full of fresh goat's milk by sundown, we'll be invited to dine with Wilbur and on the menu is us—roasted dormouse and boy stew."

"So here we are asking a drowsy, sleepy, lazy bloodhound to help us find a mason," Pip muttered to himself, slapping his forehead at Joseph's increasingly lengthy explanation.

"So, you're saying you need to find a mason to fix Tar the Troll's toppled fountain?" Red the Bloodhound wagged his tail for the first time since the visitors arrived, pleased he was able to follow Joseph's story without much difficulty while still keeping his eyes open.

"That's exactly what we need to do! Can you help us, please? Pretty please, with sugar on top?" Joseph said.

"If you promise to help us find a mason to fix Tar's fountain, then we can give fresh water to Doris the Donkey for her meadow and—"

"Yes, enough! I understand, I understood the first time!" Red shook his head. "That's an awfully long story, but don't worry, because if I can't help you find a mason, then no one can!"

Red lazily rolled off the wagon and stood tall on his hind legs. He put on an oversized blue banker's hat and tied a large white chef's apron around his waist. "Okay, let's do it!"

"Well butter my biscuit!" Pip leaned over and whispered, "Sprout, that there dog may be slower than molasses and dumber than a bucket of rocks, but he's got a heart bigger than a tractor."

Joseph sat down in the chuck wagon and ate the cured salted pork. Tired of nibbling and chewing, Pip leaned against the side of the wagon, smacked his lips, and rubbed his tummy. He looked up and saw a brilliant soap bubble floating down in a zigzag pattern above Red the Bloodhound.

Scribbles the Wizard waved at Pip and pointed to a sign in his left hand. The sign read, "Be careful of Red's directions. He mixes things up. Do the opposite of what he says."

The soap bubble floated away high up in the air and then burst, and the wizard and the bumblebee disappeared.

Joseph jumped off the chuck wagon and walked over to Pip. "What was that all about?"

"Scribbles instructed us to do just the opposite of whatever Red tells us to do."

"Did you read the sign carefully? Are you absolutely positive?"

"Sure as I'm leaning against this chuck wagon staring at a bloodhound named Red walking on his hind legs wearing a chef's apron and a banker's hat."

Red the Hound pulled a large wooden ladle from his front apron pocket, waved it in the air as if conducting an orchestra, and yelped instructions to Joseph and Pip.

"To find Mattie the Mason you must slide down that hill, climb over the rock at the bottom of the hill, skip through the hollow along the river, wade across the babbling brook at the end of the hollow, hop down the dusty trail on the other bank of the brook, tiptoe through the thorny bramble, crawl up the knoll and then dash across the meadow. There, behind the drooping cattails, you'll see the beaver dam. Then whistle three times, snap your fingers twice and shout, 'Mattie, Mattie, come out, come out wherever you are.' If you follow my directions precisely, you will find Mattie. She's the most skilled mason in all of Blackberry Bog."

Red dropped the wooden ladle in his apron pocket, leapt back in the chuck wagon, and shouted goodbye.

Joseph and Pip followed Red the Hound's directions while at the same time not forgetting Scribbles' instructions to do the opposite. They didn't slide down the hill, but climbed up. They didn't crawl over the rock, but slithered under, and at the rock at the top of the hill, not at the bottom. They ran around the hollow along the river and swam, not waded, across the babbling brook. They skipped across the dusty trail on this side of the brook, trudged around the thorny brambles, scurried down the knoll, and tiptoed past the meadow to the beaver dam behind the drooping cattails.

Soaking wet, exhausted, and anxious to meet Mattie the Mason, Pip snapped his fingers three times instead of whistling, Joseph whistled twice instead of snapping his fingers, and they both shouted, "Mattie, Mattie, come out, come out, wherever you are."

I've Been Expecting You

A pretty beaver wearing pink overalls and a white sun hat with a wide, floppy brim stood atop a mound of intertwined branches in the middle of a murky pond. She propped herself up on her big flat wide tail and waved at Joseph and Pip as they approached.

"Wow and double-wow," Pip exclaimed, gazing at the beaver. Pip stood tall in Joseph's pocket, stroked his whiskers, and put on mile-wide smile. "Look at those big, beautiful eyelashes! She's as pretty as a button!"

Mattie the Mason blushed.

"Hello there. I've been expecting you. Scribbles the Wizard told me you would be making your way to my beaver dam. Welcome, gentlemen!"

Pip's heart pounded against his ribcage and his snout twitched. Joseph waved and shouted back, "Hello there. Are you Mattie the Mason?" Awaiting a response, Joseph muttered, "I wish bug-eyed Noah could see me now! He'd be so jealous."

Pip turned to Joseph and whispered, "She's not a mason. Do you think a pretty little thing like that, cute as a button, could possibly be a mason? What's wrong with you, Sprout? She's probably an actress or a singer or a princess—but definitely not a mason. Do you think a mason would call us gentlemen?"

"Yes, I'm Mattie the Mason and this is my home," she responded. "Are you Joseph and Pip, the two travelers who were with Red the Hound—that lazy, good-hearted, faithful dog who lives in a chuck wagon? Are you the ones searching for goat's milk and fresh grass and fresh water and now a mason?"

"Yes, that's us!" Pip smiled from ear to ear and bowed. "I'm please to make your acquaintance Mattie. You sure are the prettiest mason I've ever seen."

"Why, thank you. That's the nicest thing anyone's ever said to me." Mattie lowered herself onto the mound of branches and casted her eyes downward. "You're too kind, far too kind."

"My name is Pip and this here is my friend Sprout. We would like to ask you if you would kindly follow us to Tar the Troll's fresh-water fountain. We need a mason to rebuild his toppled fountain so that we can get fresh water."

"Could you, Mattie?" Joseph pleaded. "We need fresh water to take to Doris the Donkey so she can water her meadow. She promised to give us fresh grass to give to Buffy the Billy Goat. He promised in return to give us goat's milk. Then we have to take the milk to Wilbur, the crooked old man who lives in the steeple in Zorak, and he will give Pip back his tail, and then Pip will help me find my way back to Grandpa's farm. Would you please help us, Mattie? Pretty please, with sugar on top?"

"Why, absolutely I will," Mattie the Mason responded. "And all I want in return is that cob pipe sticking out of your pyjama pocket. I've been looking for a pipe just like that one for my father."

She dove into the murky water, swam through the reeds, climbed onto a flat rock at the edge of the pond, and shook the excess water off her shiny coat.

"But where are your tools?" Joseph asked.

Mattie turned and shook her large, powerful flat tail. "This here is the only tool I need," she replied. "This here tail and a little mud will make that toppled fountain as good as new. Let's go, gentlemen. I'm right behind you."

Pip stared at her powerful tail and then turned and looked down sorrowfully at where his tail used to be.

"Don't worry Pip," Joseph said, "we'll get your tail back if it's the last thing we do."

They trudged through the meadow and scurried up the knoll. They hiked around the thorny brambles and ran across the dusty trail on this side of the brook. They dove and swam across the babbling brook and marched to the end of the hollow. Then they trekked around the hollow, slithered under the rock at the top of the hill, and ran down the other side to Tar the Troll's broken fountain.

"Okay gentlemen, give me ten minutes and the fountain will be as good as new."

Pip brought his index finger to his lips. "Shh, not too loud please. We don't want to disturb Tar the Troll again. He got very upset with us the last time. He told us that if we wake him again, we'll be tied to a stake, our eyes will be poked out with a sharp pole, our fingernails will be pulled out, our fingers and toes will be broken one by one, our ears will be pulled out of our heads, and then if we're still breathing, we'll be tickled until our hearts jump out of our months and our ribcages collapse."

"I'll be so quiet you can hear a pin drop."

Joseph and Pip watched in awe as Mattie the Mason worked relentlessly. She carried mud with her tail and began mortaring the toppled fountain back together. Inch by inch and stone by stone, the fountain grew high and higher, until it stood tall and strong. Fresh, clear water began to gush out. Joseph and Pip filled an empty barrel. They thanked the beaver again and then quietly rolled the barrel towards Doris the Donkey's meadow. Mattie the Mason propped herself on her flat, powerful tail and waved goodbye as Joseph and Pip slowly disappeared into the distance.

"Good luck, gentlemen," she shouted after them. "Thanks for the cob pipe. I'm sure Pa will love it."

A Promise Made Is a Promise Kept

Over bush and over dale, through bush and through briar, across meadow and across brook, along riverbed and along wood fence, up knoll and uphill, between bluff and between cliff, down gorge and down dusty trail, Joseph and Pip journeyed without stopping, huffing and puffing and gasping and panting, without talking, as they rolled the barrel of water to Doris the Donkey's front stoop. The thumping of hooves, the banging of doors, and the crashing of plates could be heard from inside the cottage. Joseph turned and faced the front door as it screeched open.

"Who's there?" Doris stepped out onto the porch and flicked open her red umbrella. "Is it raining yet?" She stood wide-eyed in her green galoshes and yellow raincoat. "What is that barrel doing on my property?" Before the two partners had an opportunity of introducing themselves again, Doris pranced forward and said, "Oh, I see, it's the barefooted boy and the chubby dormouse with his fingers forever plugged in his ears."

"Yes, it's us," Joseph said. "We're back with the fresh water from Blackberry Bog's old fresh-water fountain that we promised."

"Well, don't just stand there, empty the water in the meadow and let's see how long it takes for that yellow grass to turn green," Doris brayed. "Come on, don't just stand there—empty, empty. I haven't got all day!"

Joseph uncorked the barrel. The water gurgled and gushed and flowed into the meadow. The grass crackled and stretched and turned green. Within minutes, Joseph and Pip found themselves standing in a meadow of tall fresh grass. "We did it!" Joseph and Pip jumped up and down. "We did it!"

"Now you two go ahead and take as much grass as you need." Doris the Donkey turned, swung opened the door and stepped back into her home. "I can't remember *why* you asked me for the grass, but a promise made is a promise kept."

"Thanks, Doris," they said, and the donkey slammed the door closed with a thud.

Joseph carried a large sheaf of grass over a shoulder and Pip sat on Joseph's other shoulder carrying a smaller sheaf over his.

"Come on, partner, we're off to see a Billy Goat," Joseph exclaimed.

The two of them carried the sheaves up the first hill, turned right at the second windmill, and then turned left at the stable where Betsy the Cow used to live.

"I wonder where Betsy the Cow landed after she jumped over the moon." Pip shifted the sheaf of grass onto his other shoulder. "And I wonder why China the Dish decided to run away with Scoop the Spoon?"

Pip turned to Joseph and waited for some sort of answer. Joseph, thinking of home, ignored Pip's questions and trudged along the dirt road with a determined look on his face.

"Look, Pip, there's the dirt road. We only have to follow it a ways."

They walked along and listened closely for the sound of rushing water.

"In Blackberry Bog, tomorrow or yesterday doesn't exist. Today is tomorrow and yesterday is today. Tomorrow or yesterday doesn't exist. Today is tomorrow and yesterday is today."

"It's the Babbling Brook!" Pip cried out.

"That certainly is the Babbling Brook, but while time stands still in Blackberry Bog, it doesn't stand still in Zorak," Joseph reminded Pip. "If we don't hurry, Old Man Wilbur will find us and eat us for dinner. Quick, follow this dirt road down, up, down and up again. Then we should see the well."

"Beside the well there should be a sign with a yellow arrow pointing down," Pip recalled. "When we look down, we'll spot the white line painted across the path."

"Yes," Joseph said, "and once we step over that line we'll be back in Zorak!"

As they trekked towards the white line, the tall dense canopy and the old gnarled trees of the valley slowly reappeared, and the sky disappeared behind the dense canopy.

"Well, well, well. Look who's here?" Buffy the Billy Goat greeted Joseph and Pip. "If it isn't Pajama Boy and his chubby little friend with the drooping tummy!"

"That's right, Buffy. It's chubby mouse and scrawny blue eyes." Larry the Lizard stood on his hind legs and shook his head. "And what have we got here? Do I smell fresh grass?"

"Yes, it is fresh grass, and it's for you, Buffy." Joseph lifted the sheaf off his shoulder and tossed it in front of him. Pip followed. "As promised."

"Yeah, as promised!" Pip couldn't help but chime in. He wiped the mud from the bog off his orange feet and hopped into Joseph's pyjama pocket. "Now, can we please have the goat's milk you promised, so we can find our way back to Wilbur's steeple? We have a score to settle with him and then we have to find Sprout's way back home to Juniper County."

"I guess you're not quite as dumb as I thought—although you must be a card short of a deck if you're planning to go back to the steeple," Larry said.

Joseph ignored the lizard.

"Please Buffy, give us the goat's milk so we can give it back to Wilbur and he will give Pip back his tail."

"Hmmm, was that our deal? I forgot the details! Wait, I thought you were supposed to get cow's milk."

Joseph and Pip looked at each other with frowns and wide eyes.

"I'm just kidding—get it, kid-ding?" the goat said.

Joseph and Pip smiled fake smiles as Buffy trotted off into the dense forest and returned with a large jug of fresh goat's milk.

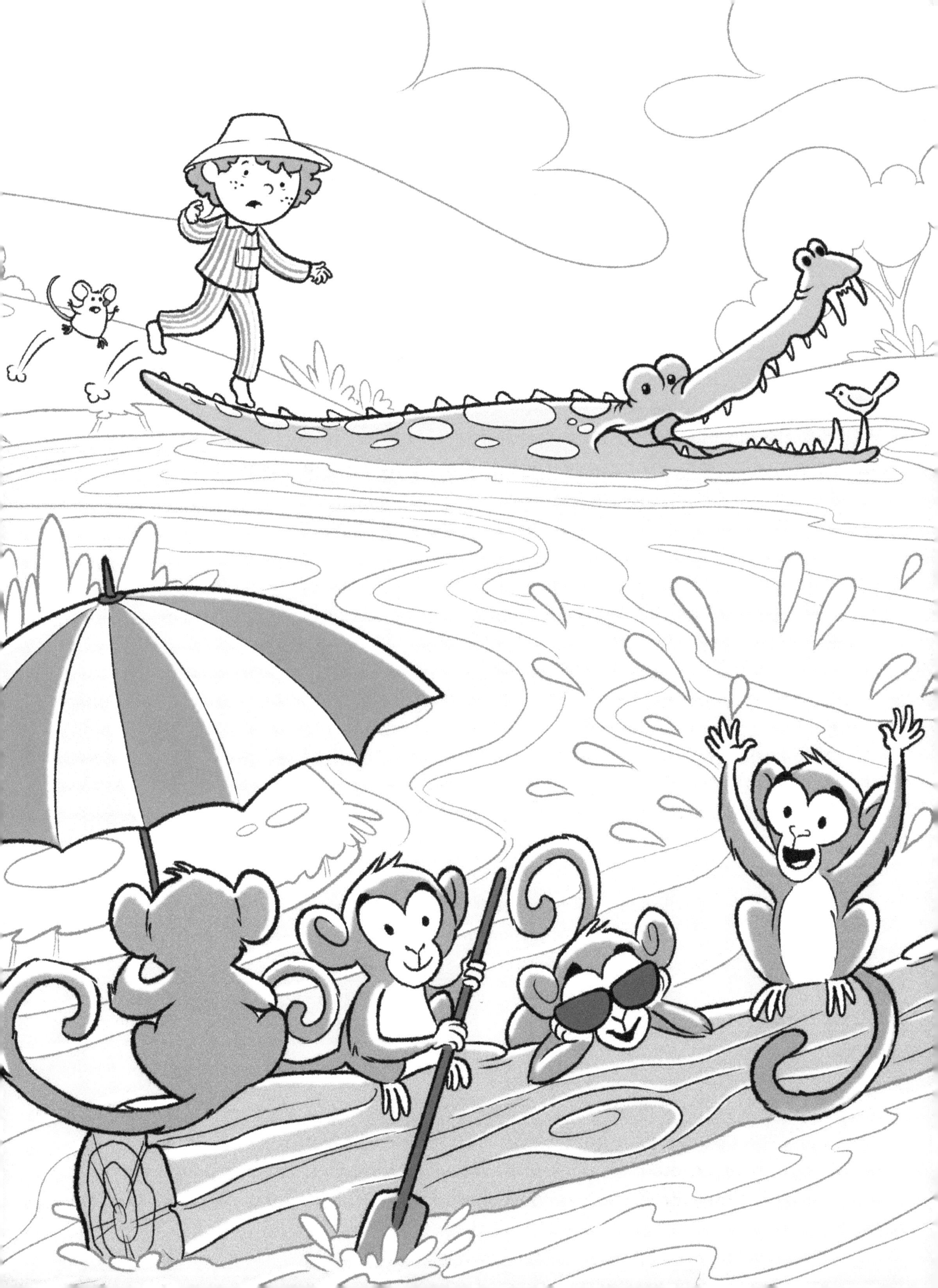

"Here you go. A deal's a deal. Now be gone!" Buffy said gruffly. "I want to chew on this fresh grass in peace. I've had enough of your long-winded stories and the long explanations about your name!"

Joseph carried the jug of goat's milk in his left hand and scurried with tail-less Pip in his front pyjama pocket towards the river's edge, closer and closer to the white line dividing Blackberry Bog and Zorak.

"Hey there Cuz. Hey there, little Blondie Blue Eyes," a familiar voice called out. "I see you've found some goat's milk."

Pip looked up at the swinging black possum with the thick black-and-white tail and the two white patches of fur around bulging red eyes staring down at him.

"Hello, Patches! Yes, we did—finally!

"But not without the help of Mattie the Mason and Tar the Troll and Doris the Donkey and Buffy the Billy Goat," Joseph added. "Mattie repaired Tar's fountain in exchange for Pip's cob pipe. Tar gave us fresh water. We gave the water to Doris to grow her yellow meadow green. Doris gave us fresh grass. We gave grass to Buffy. Buffy gave us this jug of fresh goat's milk. Now we're on our way to bring the milk to Wilbur. Then the crooked old man will give Pip back his tail."

"Then I can help Sprout find his way back to Grandpa's farm," Pip joined in.

"Well, you better hurry," Patches the Possum responded. "Allie the Alligator is on this side of Lazy River, but she won't be for long."

In the distance they could hear the banana-eating-card-playing-cigar-smoking-no-good-for-nothing mischievous monkeys chanting, "If the log rolls over, we'll all be dead! If the log rolls over, we'll all be dead!"

"I guess the monkeys are making their way across Lazy River," Joseph said as he raced to the river's edge.

"Let's find the flute in the hole in the walnut tree, call Allie the Alligator, and get back over to the Zorak side of the river," Pip urged.

"There's no need. Look!" Joseph pointed to the riverbank. "Allie is basking in the sun."

"And look!" squealed Pip. "She's about to eat that white bird perched on her front teeth!"

"Don't be silly, Pip! That bird's picking the food stuck between Allie's big, sharp teeth. That's how alligators brush their teeth."

The small white bird fluttered away and Allie snapped her large, powerful jaws shut. She floated calmly to shore. Joseph and Pip stepped onto Allie's back and both pointed towards Zorak.

"Please take us back across the river."

Allie floated past the twelve monkeys floating on the log chanting, "If the log rolls over, we'll all be dead! If the log rolls over, we'll all be dead."

Four monkeys were lying on their backs with their legs crossed and their arms tucked under their heads. Four others jumped up and down as they puffed on long, thick cigars.

The last four monkeys wearing sun hats and sunglasses kneeled on the log and paddled with their strong, powerful arms. They splashed water, cheered, and shrieked, all the while continuing their chanting and their chaotic paddling.

Pip waved at the monkeys as they floated by.

Joseph stared at the crazy monkeys and muttered, "Emma would love to see this!" He stared at Pip with a wide grin and said, "We made it, partner."

Welcome Back to Zorak

Joseph gingerly stepped off Allie the Alligator's back and onto the shore of Zorak.

"Yeah, we're almost home, but look!" Pip nosedived into Joseph's pyjama pocket, his tail-less behind sticking out and quivering in fright.

Joseph stared at a figure in the distance. "Yuk and double-yuk! I wish bug-eyed Noah could see me now! He'd be so jealous."

"Does it have two gigantic bulging white eyes with thick blue veins crisscrossing the pupils?" Pip asked.

"Yes," whispered Joseph.

"Is it bald?"

"Yes it is."

"Is its body full of oozing moles?"

"The biggest moles I've ever seen."

"And does it have the biggest, reddest, flabbiest, floppiest lips?"

"Yes it does, Pip. Along with the bonniest knees and the shortest legs and..."

"Feet as large as two frying pans?"

"If you call those paddles feet!"

"It's Ollie the Ogre! He's returned from his daily fishing trip. Be careful, Sprout!" Pip flopped around in the pyjama pocket and poked his snout out. "Look, the sun's kissing the horizon. What do we do now?"

"What do we do? We go around the stone bridge, that's what we do. We go around the stone bridge very carefully and very quietly," Joseph replied calmly. "We'll go around that grumpy, frumpy, crabby, flabby, wheezing, sneezing ogre like a hoop around a barrel."

"Right you are, partner. We don't want to end up like Hairless Felix. Remember when Henry the Hummingbird told us about that poor cat?"

"Who could forget? Poor Felix."

As the two trudged around the bridge and through the murky water, over slippery moss-covered stones and across muddy shores, they spotted the beautiful orange caterpillar with the pitch-black eyes and beautiful eyelashes curled up on a fallen log. Eight tiny black feet rested on leaves and two tiny black feet dangle above the ground. Her laced handkerchief lay beside her.

"Look, Pip—Caroline is still fast asleep."

"Shh, we mustn't disturb her Sprout." Pip stared down at her. "Ain't she beautiful?"

"She sure is."

Joseph and Pip tiptoed around the sleeping orange caterpillar as the sun continued to drop below the horizon, and then carefully crept around the bridge where Ollie remained fast asleep. They quietly trudged up an embankment and stopped to rest on a dusty dirt trail. On their right, a magnificent waterfall plunged down into a pool of crystal clear water, its cool mist blanketing the valley.

"If I remember correctly, we need to travel the path on our left," Joseph said.

"Hey, Sprout, isn't this where we saw the earth move?" Pip whispered.

"No need to whisper. I don't think Ollie the Ogre can hear us from here."

Pip hopped out of the pyjama pocket, scurried up Joseph's arm, and perched on his shoulder.

"Yes, it sure is. I remember the earth moving before my eyes." Joseph pointed to the spot. "It scared the bejeebers out of me. Can you imagine a lumbering, slumbering tortoise taking a mud bath on the second day of the month for more than 600 years?"

"Hey, do you think Old Man Wilbur's actually gonna give me back my tail?"

"I don't see why not." Joseph lifted the jug in front of his face. "After all, we did get him the goat's milk, didn't we?"

"A deal's a deal, after all!"

As they climbed farther and farther out of Blackberry Bog, the tall dense canopy and the old gnarled trees of the valley slowly reappeared. Pip pointed down at Joseph's muddy feet.

"There it is! Quick—step over the white line Sprout, and we'll finally be out of Blackberry Bog and back in Zorak!"

Joseph stepped across the white stripe and made like a long-distance runner crossing the finish line in a race.

"Hurray! It kind of feels like we're back home Sprout, doesn't it?"

"Well, I'm not anywhere close to Grandpa's farm, but in a strange way it kind of does feel like we made it back home."

They inched their way up a jagged cliff and came to rest on a green rolling hill. Pip sneezed once, twice, three times. His eyes watered. His nose twitched. "We must be near the lemon orchard Sprout. I remember making my way up this hillside before. I journeyed through the orchard to get to the steeple, and I almost sneezed the snout right off my face."

They stared at the cluster of sun baked red-clay roofed houses shimmering high atop the staggered terraces of olive trees, lemon trees, and vineyards. Half of the bright orange sun floated above the horizon.

"Look up there," Pip pointed. "There's Wilbur's steeple."

Familiar jagged cliffs, smooth rock faces, regal blue pine, and clusters of cypress trees blanketed the majestic mountain range beyond Wilbur's steeple.

"Let's get cracking, Sprout! We've got a crooked old man waiting for his goat's milk to visit... and he has my beautiful tail. Then I'll help you find a way back to Grandpa's farm—wherever that is."

"What a dream—a fantastic dream!" Joseph cried out and patted Pip on top of the head.

"Let's get a move on Pajama Boy, Sir Joseph," Pip joked.

"Hey, you forgot 'Fella' and 'Gentleman,' " Joseph said.

They had an ear-to-ear grin as they walked along the path towards the steeple. Pip rested on Joseph's shoulder and Joseph swung the jug of fresh goat's milk. They stopped at the fence where Joseph crashed into when he first landed in Zorak.

"Hey Sprout do remember that fence?"

"How could I possibly forget?"

Pip jumped on top of Joseph's head and waved his arms in the air like a conductor at a symphony, prepared for Joseph's recounting of his harrowing journey into Zorak.

"I think I came crashing and smashing into that fence, after zooming and zipping down a hillside, after swooshing and whooshing down a snow-covered peak, barrelling fast and faster down the mountain, dodging large boulders, sliding over frozen streams and under giant cedars, and ploughing through giant snow banks. The snow beneath me suddenly disappeared and I rolled like a barrel down a steep cliff, bumping and scraping along the ground, after floating and fluttering down a shaft filled with bright light, after bumping and banging down a dark tunnel, after thumping and thudding down a hole in Grandpa's magical cavern, after tumbling and fumbling into this crazy dream, after watching a falling star in the night sky and wishing, "Star light, star bright, the first star I see tonight; I wish I may, I wish I might, have the wish I wish tonight," after plopping into bed, after gobbling garbanzo beans roasted in magical sand in Grandpa's fire pit."

"And then you met me." Pip pointed at himself. "If I remember correctly, I was swinging from a garland of garlic above a pudgy tomcat who just so happened to be the pet of the crooked old man who we have to see before sundown." Pip jumped back into Joseph's pyjama pocket. "Let's get a move on. I don't intend to be on Wilbur's menu this evening and I want my beautiful pencil-thin pink tail back."

The Tale of the Return of the Tail

The lone window in the steeple was open to the cool evening air. Old Man Wilbur, his stomach rumbling and grumbling, stood by the shelf and pointed to the can of beans, two onions, and half-loaf of bread.

"Eeny, meeny, miny, moe, catch a child by the toe, if *he* hollers, don't let *him* go, eeny, meeny, miny, moe," he chanted. "Eeny, meeny, miny, moe, catch a child by the toe, if *she* hollers, don't let *her* go, eeny, meeny, miny, moe."

The crooked old man's gnarled finger stopped at the half-loaf of mouldy bread.

"I hate stale bread!" he growled.

Then he pointed to the onions and can of beans.

"Eeny, meeny, miny, moe, catch *many* children by the toe, if *they* holler, don't let *them* go, eeny, meeny, miny, moe." His old gnarled finger stopped at the onions.

"Onions make me cry," he snarled.

Wilbur stared at the can of beans.

"I'd rather eat a little boy or a little girl!"

He smacked his lips, picked up the can of beans, and turned towards his rickety rocking chair.

"Wait a minute! It's almost sundown. If that foolish child and his chubby little friend don't get here in the next fifteen minutes, they'll be on tonight's menu—roasted dormouse and boy stew...yum and double-yum!"

Wilbur tossed the can of beans back on the shelf and inserted his fat fingers behind the straps of his overalls. He picked up a butternut squash from the wooden chest, popped it in his mouth, and then stomped across the steeple to the open window. He leaned out, crunching and chewing, then spit out one, two, three, four, five seeds. He plucked a long, wiry hair from his nostril as he surveyed the valley down below.

"Well, well, well," he shouted. "Speak of the devils."

Joseph lingered at the bottom of the steeple's front stoop as Pip stood in his pyjama pocket.

"I smell goat's milk—fresh, tasty goat's milk," Wilbur roared, spitting more seeds out the window.

"Look out, Sprout! Wilbur's spitting seeds again."

Startled by the commotion, Acorn lifted her head, yawned, and turned towards the wall to continue her late afternoon nap.

"Hello up there Mr. Wilbur. We're back with the goat's milk you asked for." Joseph held the jug up in the air.

"Give me my goat's milk, you morsel of a boy!"

"Hurry, Sprout! We haven't much time—look, the sun has almost set."

"Yes, hurry, hurry, hurry," tweeted Do, Re and Mi as they fluttered above Joseph's head, their long yellow scarves trailing behind them.

"Get a move on it, you two fools!" Larry the Lizard shouted, scurrying up the wall of the steeple and nestling in a shallow crack. He stared down at Pip and Joseph, shaking his head in amazement. "I can't believe you two dummies are still in one piece."

"Wait, don't go through that door kid, you won't make your way back out," warned Buffy the Billy Goat, butting his head on a fallen log lying at the side of the dirt road, and glaring up at the window. "Hey Wilbur, a promise is a promise." *Butt!* "The sun is just about to set and they made it back in time." *Butt!* "Throw down Chubby's tail and I'll see to it that they leave your jug of fresh goat's milk by the landing." *Butt!* "And no funny stuff."

Wilbur, grunting and groaning and spitting and drooling, plucked another long, wiry hair from his prominent nose and flung it out the window. He stomped his feet. The walls of the steeple crackled and trembled and rumbled and rattled. The bell in the belfry began to clang and clink and jangle. The crooked old man leaned out over the windowsill and dangled the pencil-thin pink tail in the air.

"Drop it, drop it!" tweeted Do, Re, and Mi, frantically fluttering above Joseph's head, sending feathers flying to the ground.

"A promise is a promise Wilbur," Joseph reminded the crooked old man.

"I'll fool them," Wilbur whispered over his shoulder to Acorn, beginning to think up a scheme. "I'll have me goat's milk *with* roasted dormouse and boy stew tonight for dinner."

He grinned and bent out the window, still holding Pip's tail high in the air, and yelled out, "Meet me at the door with the jug of goat's milk and I'll hand over the mouse's tail."

Wilbur started to bend his head back inside the window intending to grab both the jug of goat's milk and Joseph and Pip at the front door, when everyone standing outside the steeple saw an orange blur land on the crooked old man's backside, followed by an ear-splitting screech.

"Look, it's Acorn!" Joseph shouted. "He's jumped on Wilbur!"

Wilbur bolted upright from Acorn's weight, the back of his head hit the window frame, and Pip's tail slipped out of his spade-like hand, spinning and tumbling, flip-flopping fast and faster to the ground, and finally landed at Joseph's feet.

Pip winced at the sight of his tail hitting the ground. "Ouch, that hurt!" He hopped out of Joseph's pyjama pocket and scurried over to pick it up. "I got my tail back, I got my tail back Sprout!" Pip turned and delicately re-joined his tail to his plump behind, and then he scuttled back up to Joseph's shoulder. He rubbed his snout up against Joseph's cheek. "We did it!"

"We did indeed, Pip."

"Thank you partner. I would never have got my tail back without you." Pip stared back at his tail swaying happily to and fro. "What a beautiful pink tail I have. It's *absolutely*, breathtakingly beautiful, isn't it, Sprout?"

"It's the most stunning, most attractive, most striking pink tail I've ever seen partner!"

"Never ever return to my steeple," Wilbur thundered as he rubbed his head amid the crackling and trembling and rumbling and rattling and the clanging and clicking and jangling and the butting.

When the crowd spotted Acorn emerging from an opened lower window, loud cheers rang out.

"Old Man Wilbur wasn't going to play fair," Acorn, shouted over their hurrahs. "He was going to keep the goat's milk *and* eat the little boy with the straw hat and missing front teeth and the fat mouse for dinner. It doesn't bother me that the crooked old man eats boy and girls, but I can't stomach it when someone doesn't keep their word. That's where I draw the line."

Wilbur pulled his head back inside and slammed the window closed. The crackling and trembling and rumbling and clanging and jangling and butting stopped. Everyone stared up at the window in silence.

Larry the Lizard finally broke the silence. "You two best be on your way," he told Joseph and Pip. "You've caused enough trouble in these parts to last a lifetime, and it's getting dark." He looked to Buffy the Billy Goat sitting on the fallen log and then back to Joseph and Pip. "You're lucky to be alive. Why, if you two fell into a pool of manure, you'd come out smelling like roses. It's best if you were gone—forever. Hurry, before your luck runs dry and that crooked old man changes his mind and decides to chase you and have roasted dormouse and boy stew after all."

Let's Give It a Try

Delighted that Pip got his tail back, happy to begin their journey back to Grandpa's farm, yet sad at having to leave all his new friends behind, Joseph trudged down the path toward the fence. His shoulders drooped and his head slouched forward. He stopped, turned, and faced the steeple one last time. With tears in his eyes, he waved goodbye to the three swallows. Do removed his top hat and bowed, Re removed his white gloves and waved, and Mi covered his face in the yellow scarf and wept.

"Goodbye friends, and thanks for everything," Joseph said in a trembling voice. "We're off to find the path to Grandpa's farm."

Pip stood tall in Joseph's pyjama pocket, smacked his forehead, and mouthed, "How in the devil are we supposed to find the path to Grandpa's farm?"

He shrugged, slumbered back to the bottom of the pocket, and curled up into a ball.

"Hey Pip, you can't go to sleep now. We have to start looking. Get on up on my shoulder and help me find the way back home, will ya?"

Pip popped out of Joseph's pyjama pocket, raced over to Joseph's shoulder, and stood at attention. "Aye-aye, Captain Sprout!" he saluted. "Private Pip at your service, sir!"

Then he held his hands and arms out in front of his face as if he were holding a pirate spyglass. "Straight ahead, Captain! I think I spot the fence down below!"

"I've never been called Captain before." Joseph strode quickly towards the fence. "I've been called all sorts of names on this extraordinary adventure. My real name is Joseph, but my family and friends call me Sprout, and some call me G.I. Joe on account of my khaki-coloured overalls with the army logo stamped on them. My dad sewed them for me." Joseph looked down at his striped pyjamas and then back up at Pip. "My brothers have called me different names, but never Captain, although recently I was called Squirt by Red the Hound. Tar the Troll called me Silly Boy. Doris the Donkey called me Barefooted Boy. Patches the Possum called me Blondie Blue Eyes. Caroline the Caterpillar called me Wilbur. You, Pip, who smokes a cob pipe like my Pa, called me Sleepy Head and Virgil. The *real* Wilbur called me Morsel. Do, Re and Mi the singing swallows with top hats and yellow scarves called me Sir Joseph. Acorn the Tomcat who wears an orange-and-purple striped tie with four different coloured sneakers called me Kid. Buffy the Billy Goat with a long white beard and dark-rimmed glasses called me Pajama Boy. Larry the Lizard called me Dumb for entering the steeple. Grandpa once called me Tadpole. But I was never called Captain."

Pip had plugged his ears and stared at Joseph.

"Private Pip? Hey, Pip!"

Pip pulled his fingers out. "Sorry partner… I mean, Captain. I just couldn't bear to listen. I think I'd go madder than a wet hen if I had to listen to that one more time."

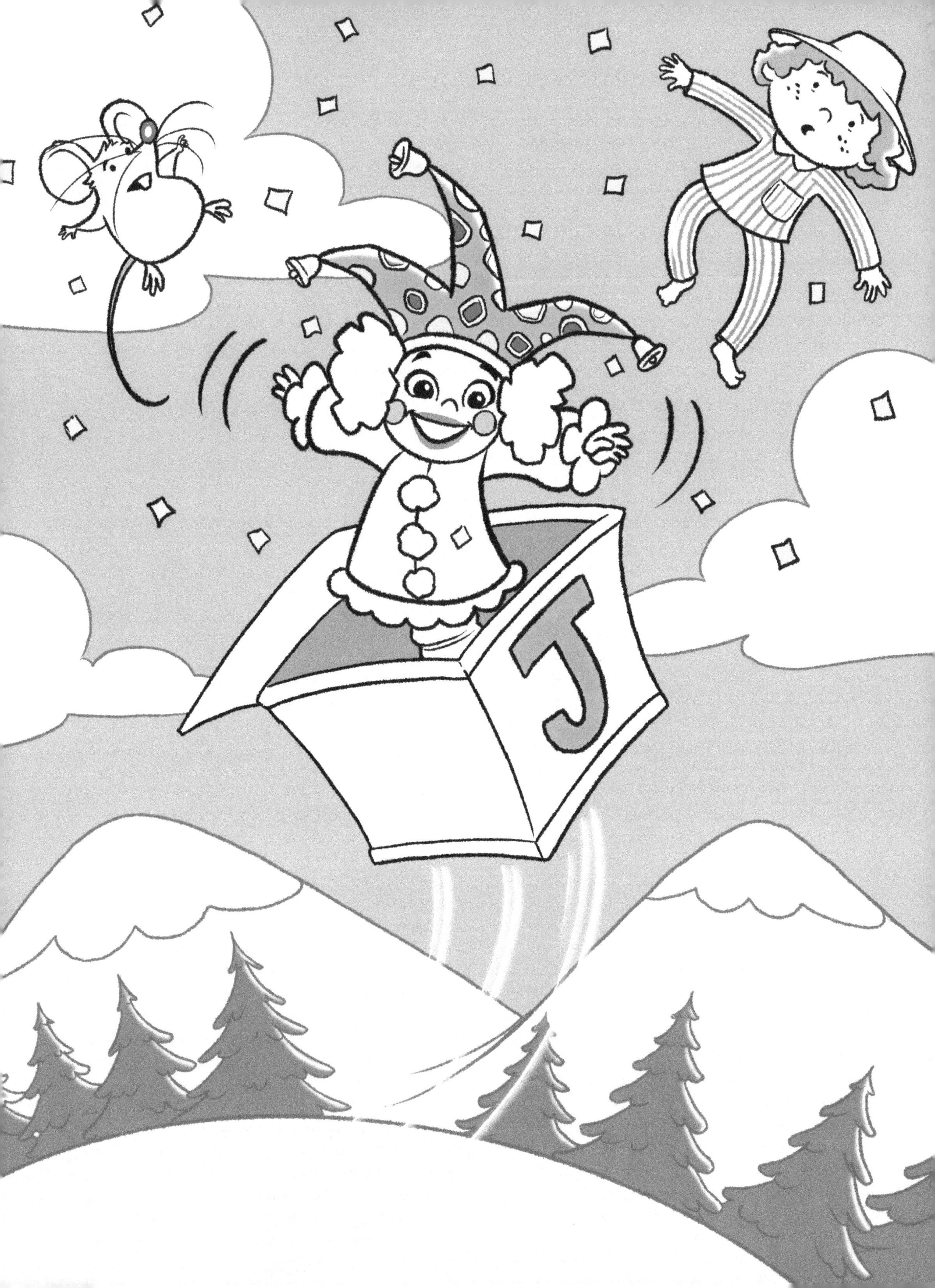

Joseph laughed and patted Pip on the head.

"I guess I *have* been repeating myself?" Joseph lifted Pip off his shoulder and placed him back in his front pocket. "Now let's find our way back to Grandpa's farm, Private. We've got a warm, cozy bed waiting for us."

Pip's stomach grumbled and rumbled. "I think I could do with some delicious roasted garbanzo beans right about now. They have a *special* ingredient, right Sprout?" Pip winked up at Joseph.

"Look, down there," Joseph pointed to the fence and a big wide grin swept across his face. "I think I came crashing and smashing into this fence, after zooming and zipping down a hillside, after swooshing and whooshing down a snow-covered peak, barrelling fast and faster down the mountain, dodging around large boulders, sliding over frozen streams and under giant cedars, and ploughing through giant snow banks. The snow beneath me suddenly disappeared and I rolled like a barrel down a steep cliff, bumping and scraping along the ground, after floating and fluttering down a shaft filled with bright light, after bumping and banging down a dark tunnel, after thumping and thudding down a hole in Grandpa's magical cavern, after tumbling and fumbling into this crazy dream, after watching a falling star in the night sky and saying, 'Star light, star bright, the first star I see tonight; I wish I may, I wish I might, have the wish I wish tonight, after plopping into bed, after gobbling garbanzo beans roasted in magical sand in Grandpa's fire pit."

Sprout looked down at Pip and then covered his mouth with the open palm of his hand. "Oops, sorry Pip. I'm doing it again ain't I?"

Pip pointed to a brilliant soap bubble floating overhead.

"Look, its Scribbles, the silent bronco-busting wizard who rides a pet bumblebee. Read the sign, Sprout! Read the sign!"

Joseph looked up and squinted at the message. He read it out loud.

"To get back to Grandpa's farm you must talk to the jack-in-the-box. But first you must find Stella the Shooting Star who arches through the night sky immediately after sunset."

The brilliant soap bubble floated away into the night sky and popped, and Scribbles the Wizard and Billy the Bumblebee disappeared.

Pip sat up in Joseph's pyjama pocket, smacked his forehead, and mouthed, "How on earth are we ever going to find a jack-in-the-box in the dark?"

Joseph leaned against the fence, scratched his head, and stared up at the twinkling stars.

"Well this certainly is something," he said. "A wizard riding a bumblebee claiming he'll show me the way home, and now waiting for a shooting star named Stella to find a jack-in-the-box."

A whistling, screeching noise like fingernails scraping against slate startled Joseph.

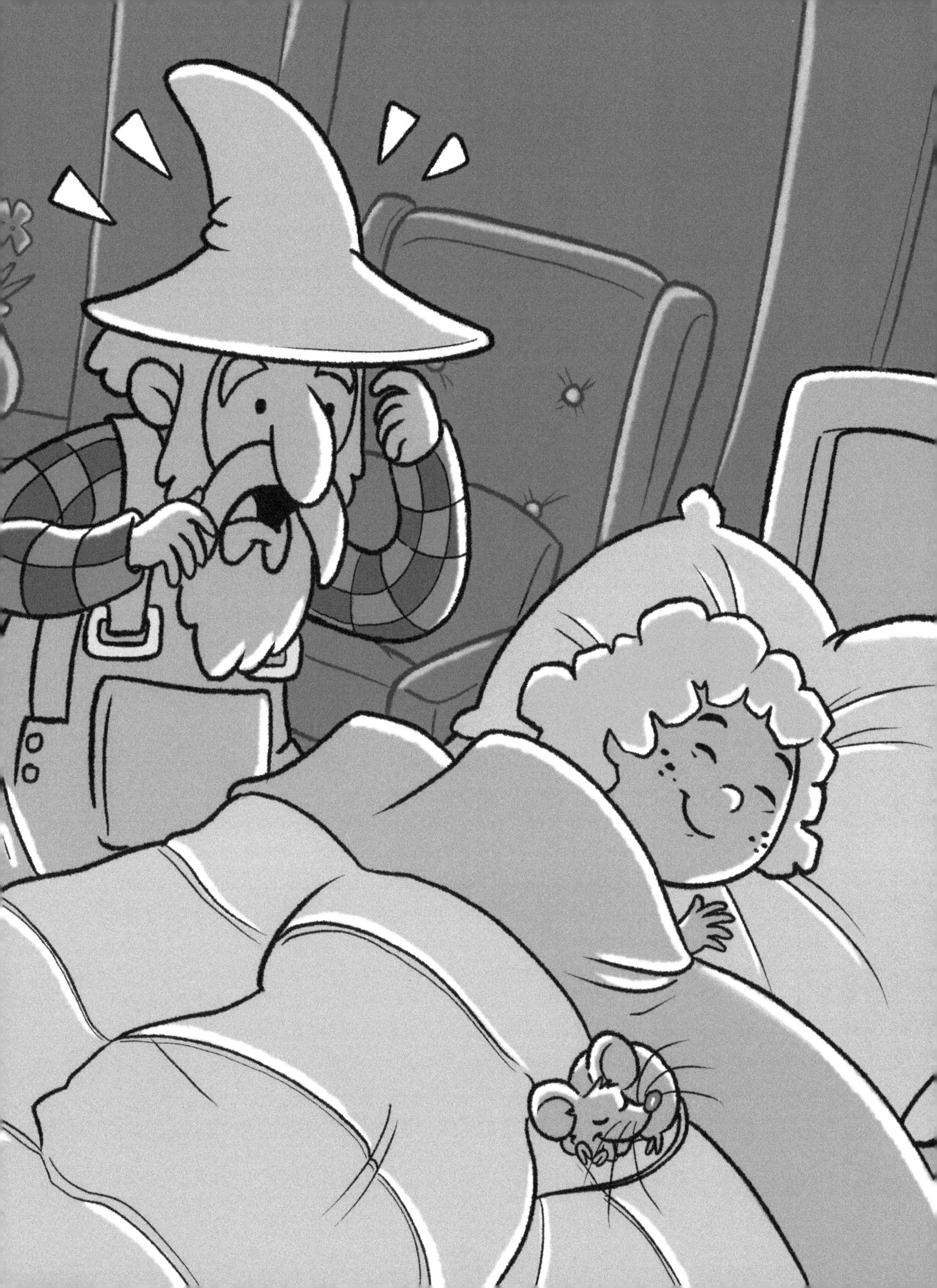

"Look, there, behind you, Captain!" Pip squealed. "It's a shooting star streaking across the night sky... it's Stella!"

"Hey, Stella!" they shouted. "Stop!"

The star arched rapidly across the sky leaving a trail of sparkling stardust in its wake, and landed behind a small hill. A brilliant bright light illuminated the land.

"Come on, Captain!" Pip pulled on Joseph's pyjama shirt. "We have a star named Stella to speak with."

As the two tiptoed towards the fallen star, a brilliant blue light engulfed them.

"Hey, Captain, you're blue, just like me," Pip chuckled.

Joseph shielded his eyes with his arms. "Hello there, are you Stella?" Staring in awe and awaiting a reply, Joseph muttered, "Emma would love to see this!"

"Yes, I'm Stella the Shooting Star. Scribbles wrote all about you and your chubby little friend and all about your marvellous adventure that took up many, many signs."

The light faded and then glowed bright again.

"I remember you. You're the one who made that wish behind the bedroom window. Yes, you're the one. I'd recognize those blue eyes and carrot-coloured curly hair and those freckles anywhere!"

The star's light faded then glowed brightly again. "Smile for me, will you? Then I'll know for sure."

Joseph smiled wide.

"Yup, that's you! The missing front teeth give it away."

"Can you help us get back home Stella?" Joseph asked.

"If I can't help you... then nobody can! The jack-in-the-box is waiting for you around that pond. Now run along! If the jack-in-the-box decides to shut down, she can sleep for months at a time, you may never get back home."

"Come on Pip, we've got a jack-in-the-box to meet up with. Let's get a move on!" Joseph waved to the pulsating blue light. "Thanks for everything Stella."

The two partners wore big smiles as they quickly trekked around the pond.

"Stop! If you topple me, my lid will jam shut and I won't be able to help you."

Joseph halted, thinking "I wish bug-eyed Noah could see me now! He'd be so jealous."

"Wow, I thought you were going to plough right into me. Thank heavens you stopped!" exclaimed a pretty little court jester, attached to a spring inside a large yellow box with the letter J on the front, bouncing up and down. "Hello, I'm Jackie."

Pip stared at Jackie's three-peaked hat with a patchwork of red, green, and blue diamonds. A silver bell jingled at the end of each drooping peak. Her cheeks and lips looked bright red. Her big, round green eyes stared but never blinked. "J is for Jackie and Jester and Jack."

"We want to get back to Grandpa's farm. Can you help us?" asked Joseph.

"*Us?* What do you mean *us?*" Jackie the Court Jester laughed. "Scribbles had said that *a young boy* needed to get back home. That's you. Why are you saying *us?*"

The smiles quickly faded from Pip's and Joseph's faces. The chubby little mouse's eyes filled with tears. He hopped out of Joseph's front pyjama pocket and onto the soft, moist ground. He plodded away from his friend, head held low, floppy ears waddling to and fro, his re-joined tail dragging behind him.

"Hey wait, Pip, Pipster, Private, Partner. Where are you going? Stop right there," Joseph shouted. "That's an order!"

Pip turned and stared up at the boy in the striped pyjamas and curly hair the colour of carrots and the deep blue eyes and the freckles and the missing front teeth.

"Goodbye, my friend, forever and ever, goodbye." Pip choked back his tears and turned away from Joseph.

"Hi-ho, Hi-ho, it's off to *eat* I go!" he blubbered, sobbing at the top of his lungs.

"Wait, stop right there! Hush a moment so I can think." Joseph wiped tears from his eyes. "You're not… I mean, we're not… I mean, I'm not going anywhere without you Pip. Not now, not tomorrow, not ever. Hop back into my pyjama pocket. That's an order, Private!"

Pip turned, forced a smile, and waved his tiny orange hand in the air.

"Goodbye, my friend. Goodbye, forever."

"What's eating you? I'm not going anywhere without you, understood? Now get back in my pocket!"

Joseph turned to Jackie the Court Jester and whispered, "Thank you, Jackie. I really appreciate all your help, but I'm not going anywhere without that chubby, droopy, fury, floppy-eared, pencil-thin-tailed mouse. I'm staying in Zorak with Pip." Joseph pivoted and lumbered behind Pip with his head hanging low and his shoulders drooping.

"Wait a second." Jackie started to bounce. "If your chubby friend stays nestled in the front pocket of your pyjamas, I think the both of you could fit inside the box."

"Really, do you think it's possible?" Joseph's voice quivered.

"I've never done it before. But let's give it a try! Now get on in here and don't waste another second."

Pip jumped into Joseph's front pyjama pocket elated. "Let's get a move on. Grandpa's waiting for us Captain!"

Joseph hopped, skipped, and somersaulted right into the box. "Off we go!"

Laughing and bouncing, Jackie the Court Jester slowly recoiled into the box and then announced, "Okay folks, you're on a one-way ticket to Grandpa's farm. Once the lid snaps shut, on the count of seven, both of you will be catapulted straight to Grandpa's farmhouse—no stopping, no washroom breaks, no detours, and no need to thank me. You'll find yourself snuggled under a warm, toasty blanket in your own bedroom in seven-six-five-four…"

"Wait, wait. One last question before we go. Why are we counting down from seven? Why not from three?" Joseph asked.

"Don't be silly, Sprout! How many days are there in a week?"

Jackie continued her count. "Three-two-one!" She shut the lid and then it sprang back open, catapulting Joseph and Pip into the night sky.

"Goodbye and happy trails!"

Home at last

They soared up above hills and steep cliffs and giant cedars and giant snow banks. They hurled over snow-capped peaks and majestic mountain ranges. They shot up a shaft of white light and through a dark tunnel and then a sandy shaft and softly land in... Grandpa's magical cavern.

"Am I alive? Where am I? What about my tail?" Pip dusted off his blue-grey fur and shook in fright. "Where are you, Sprout?"

"We're here, Pip!" Joseph reached for Pip's little orange hand. "We're in Grandpa's cavern. Look there, behind that boulder. It's Grandpa's coalminer's lantern and it's still glowing. We're back home! Yippy! Hurrah! Hurrah!"

"Hey, wait a minute." Pip climbed up on Joseph's shoulder and looked toward the boulder. "Didn't that springing, bouncing, leaping, laughing jack-in-the-box say that we would be in your bed under a warm, toasty wool blanket?"

Joseph broke out in laughter.

"I guess you were too heavy to complete the journey, my chubby little friend. But at least we made it back to Grandpa's cavern. Don't worry. I promise you'll be snuggling under a warm, toasty wool blanket soon enough."

Joseph lifted the lantern above his head. Spangles of red, green, orange, blue, and white light frightened Pip. He hopped into Joseph's pyjama pocket with only his twitching nose sticking out.

"I wonder if any pirates, wizards, dragons, ogres, or fairies live in this cavern," Pip said, his voice echoing in the cavern.

"We've got no time to think about that right now. We've got to get back to Grandpa's farm. Besides, haven't you had enough adventure Private Pip?"

"Lead the way, Captain Sprout."

Joseph hiked down the horse trail, through the hollow, between the rock bluffs, along the river, up the slope to the willow tree, through the pumpkin patch, and past the fire pit.

"We're home, Pip," Joseph whispered. "We're finally and truly home."

Pip nestled deep inside the pyjama pocket as Joseph tiptoed through the front door of the farmhouse and down the hallway. He noticed the half-filled bag of magical sand resting on the mantle of the hearth. He pushed open his bedroom door and then slipped under the warm, toasty wool blanket on his bed.

"Good night Pip," Joseph whispered. "Sleep tight and don't let the bedbugs bite." Joseph stared at his new furry friend and muttered, "Emma would love to hear about this... and bug-eyed Noah would be so jealous!"

"Good night Sprout." Pip curled up on the pillow beside Joseph's head and snuggled up against his cheek. "Sweet dreams."

Advice on Reading
Magical Adventures

The next morning, Seth heard Grandpa and his parents in Joseph's bedroom. He pushed open the door and saw them standing around Joseph's bed talking about how Joseph had woken up mumbling incoherently about fanciful things—talking animals with odd names wearing fancy clothes, strange lands with strange names and even stranger landscapes, about falling down a tunnel and tumbling down a snow-covered mountain, repeating the names of girls like Stella and Jackie and Lauren and Caroline and Doris and Emma, and something about magical garbanzo beans and an enchanted cavern.

Ma, wiping tears from her eyes, cried out that her poor little Joey was feverish and terribly ill, and she wanted to call for the doctor. Then she said that perhaps it was just growing pains. Pa muttered that he always warned Tadpole that too many magical fairy tales and adventurous comics could lead a boy to hallucinations and gibberish and daydreaming and even nightmares.

After everyone had gone, Grandpa remained sitting quietly beside Joseph's bed, with a strange smile on his face, holding a chubby little mouse up in the air by the tip of its tail.

CPSIA information can be obtained
at www.ICGtesting.com
Printed in the USA
LVHW071519280220
648532LV00014B/1001

9 781528 908351